A Fe[...]
Many Colours

Lyn Benzino

Fruit Salad
Press

Published in 2022 by Fruit Salad Press

Copyright © Lyn Benzino 2022

Lyn Benzino has asserted her right to be identified as the author of this Work
in accordance with the Copyright, Designs and Patents Act 1988

ISBN Paperback: 978-1-7397007-0-6
Ebook: 978-1-7397007-1-3

A CIP catalogue copy of this book can be found in the British Library.

Published with the help of Indie Authors World
www.indieauthorsworld.com

IndieAuthors
World

For all my family and friends who accept me as I am.

For Liz Potts – thank you for your invaluable help.

You can tell your own story, you can create your own truth, and you can show your own light. You can think and control your own destiny.

The only trouble is that it takes courage, faith, and belief in the truth to be able to access a connection to the Universal Energy. We all have this within us.

We have to go through hard work, darkness, grief, suffering, and adversity to be able to see the comparison of love, happiness, joy, and spirituality.

Introduction

This is my story. It is complex, but has a profound simplicity within it.

To be able to be happy seems the easiest concept, and yet it is, or can seem, a difficult pathway to tread. You would ideally want happiness to be as simple as it sounds. Thus far, it has been seen by me and many before me on multiple occasions, although not entirely captured. When one has the knowledge and the skill to know how happiness can be achieved, but nevertheless it still eludes them, then this is a difficult burden to bear – the guilt which comes with knowing the answer, but not being able to solve the puzzle. And the frustration that consumes me when I know how to feel happiness… yet I have not been able to achieve this feeling for long periods of time. I am not alone in this. Many people with the skills, intelligence, and natural ability to have this within their power, to be able to fully let their light shine from within, are unable to sustain this feeling for any length of time. Still, there are those who can do this very same thing without struggling. Or so it seems.

I am going to tell you something now, something that you may have read in fairy tales, something that you may have seen in films, something that you might think dreams are made of. Something that has been happening since the beginning of time. We at times may think we know a lot. We have brief synapses of light bestowed upon us. But in comparison to wisdom's ages, we know only a tiny piece of this great jigsaw which is life. Wisdom does not advance by generation as technology does, because technology can be passed on as fact, but wisdom can only be learned by experience and feeling. The average physical human's lifespan is 79 years. You would think that would be long enough – and maybe it is for some.

This story is fantastic, this story is perfect, this story is simple, yet profoundly complex. This story is spiritual, and this story is true… except for the bits that are not.

1

Flying

…I was flying! But the take-off was not an easy one. Where a bird would run a little, flapping their wings and then take flight, I had to find a large outdoor space where no-one would see me for at least a few minutes. Then I would run a short distance and jump as high as I could, and keep repeating this process until I was airborne. It helped me view life from a higher perspective. When I was airborne, it took a lot of effort to stay up in the air. I had to keep pushing my legs, like I was doing breaststroke, to be able to stay up. It wasn't easy, but I loved it. It was exciting to be flying and skimming the rooftops, where I was able to see all life below – friends, family, or strangers. I was visiting them, but they didn't realise, and I could see through their walls, through brick, through tile and slate, and know how they felt and what they were doing…

But on this occasion, something felt different. I was in a fog; a twisted fog. Am I right, or am I wrong? Am I here, or am I there? I felt the cold surround my internal organs; I felt the shape and size of them. My mood had changed from enjoyment to confusion, to the stinging chill of fear.

What was that in the distance? I squinted through the haze, barely making out a figure ahead. I am usually alone in these excursions. This was not right! The decision to follow brought a shiver right through me, even though I felt I had no choice in the matter. I needed to breathe. I exhaled loudly, with force, then took a big gulp of air. Phew, that felt better, and now there seemed to be some sun trying to shine through the greyness.

Then a face appeared inches from mine! Our eyes locked together as it understood my darkest dreams. The pressure was immense. My skin felt like it could be ripped off at any moment! The feather on my back was being pulled away. I couldn't let it be taken away from me. I had to get back on solid ground!

…I must have fallen asleep for a moment, because I missed the end of the programme.

**

Here I am, wishing spring then summer would arrive, and it is only January! Me of all people! I have never wanted to wish time away! I have always preferred Mondays, the beginning of things, the start of the film, the start of the story, getting ready for a party, the start of a holiday… I do not usually want time to go any more quickly, for time is precious and even more so now than ever!

'*It's Friday!*' the DJ on the radio was spouting.

When people wish for the end of the week, always on about 'it's Fridaaay!', it irritates me immensely! When people say they are bored and just waiting for the weekend to begin, I don't understand how that can be possible! Time to me is never to be wished away 'willy nilly'; it's always been too valuable to me. Throughout my life, I have felt distressed when I heard others say that they wish that some event, or some future period of time in the year or in their life, would come sooner. I felt almost a sort of panic that their wishes could speed up time, and it concerned me even as a youngster. Looking back makes me wonder, *Did I know then that there was so much to fit into my life? And did I know that the process would seem so incredibly slow, and that the task would be tremendously intricate?*

It was raining again, back to the drizzle after a few days of bitter cold sunshine, frost, and ice. It was milder and wetter today; well, at least I didn't have to scrape the ice off the car this morning, which meant I could have an extra ten minutes in bed! My feather ached; it felt raw, like a tattoo that had not long been inked in! Not that I have ever knowingly had a tattoo! It's just what I imagine it would feel like.

I have never been able to remember the moment that the feather was tattooed on my back, because for as long as I can remember, it has always been there. When I was very young, I never really thought about why it was there, nor who or what had made it appear. I suppose when you grow up in a certain way, or as a certain person, then you assume that everyone else is the same – until you're older and know more of the world and other people's lives and feelings. I thought that all people saw and felt things as I did – except for the bad stuff, of course! Only the good I thought others knew; only the things that made me happy did I imagine others shared. The bad things in my mind, I assumed others did not have. But I never really thought about the fact that I had this mark. Perhaps I just reckoned everyone else did, too.

Getting up and dressed was more of a struggle than usual this morning. My legs felt like lead, and I was disgruntled to say the least. As I walked through my working day, I was astonished to find that the people I met during this time all represented, in some small way, a piece of me reflected back. It was like looking in the mirror, only sometimes I did not like what I saw. But then there were moments when I saw beauty reflected right back at me and could see myself shining through others!

I knocked on a door – a rather scruffy turquoise door with a scuffed area which the knocker had worn down over the years. There was silence. I knocked again, and moments later a clumsy noise came bumping down the stairs. It was an only-just-woke-up kind of noise. When the occupant eventually came to the door, after awkwardly attempting to get the keys in the lock a few times, it was obvious in just one glance that last night had been a lively experience for him. The clues were all there; I only needed seconds to scan, and in what seemed like an instant, I knew! The pizza all over his face from the night before, a smothered tomato base spread all round his mouth and on the side of his face – that ravenous hunger that only comes with too many alcoholic beverages! Ha! His hair was dishevelled, and he was fully dressed in the crumpled clothes he appeared to have worn all the previous day. He was too much in a daze to be embarrassed about the way he looked, and I had seen it all before. I handed him the parcel, and he thanked me automatically.

As the day developed, I began to feel more relaxed and energetic. As I trundled down the hill, a car pulled up by the side of me, as they often do, the occupant asking for directions or a parcel, or something they are expecting which hasn't arrived. Except this time it was a friend of mine, Elsie. She looked perturbed about something, but we were pleased to see each other. She said she was on her way to her textile course, but I often saw her driving round this area, and even though she lived only a few streets away from where she had stopped, I couldn't help thinking that she hadn't chosen a very direct route to where she was going.

'Have you seen "His Nibs"?' Elsie enquired in a rather agitated way.

Before I could answer, she demanded, 'Have you EVER seen him around here'?

'No,' I lied.

I felt a sharp pain in my shoulder blade. But I couldn't tell the truth, could I? Elsie would blow her top and possibly do something that would get her arrested, or worse! No… No, she could kill if unhinged! Best stay quiet and think about whether to tell her the truth at a later date. I thought about her and the partner she had been seeing for all these years, and wondered how someone so intelligent and with so much going for them could be taken in by a totally self-indulgent, egotistical, narcissistic, hedonist like him! But they say love is blind! Never a truer word spoken! They had split up so many times, yet somehow, she always gave into his charms.

But he didn't have any, as far as I was concerned.

I told myself not to judge, and carried on with my day. I needed to get finished on time, as I wanted to get to the shops to look for a new table lamp. The rest of my shift progressed without any further interruptions, and I was able to get home, have a quick cup of coffee, and get changed before the shops shut.

In the queue at the shop, the lady in front of me was taking something back, and I waited impatiently for my turn, while children played by the door. The woman was returning a phone, and I watched the way the cashier was dealing with the refund, and the way the woman was watching the children to make sure they didn't run out of the shop. In my head, I was questioning how the refund worked, wondering what the woman was going to do without a phone, and how it seemed to be such a complicated transaction. I felt the growing impatience of the person standing behind me in the queue, the closeness of their body infringing on my personal space. I was also aware of the apparent speed of the parallel queue to my right, and the huddle of the people waiting to pick up their parcels.

Blimey! What was in that cup of coffee?

I arrived home with my new lamp and put it on my side table in the living room. It looked lovely, and it made the room seem cosy in the evening when I sat with a cup of tea or watched the telly without the glare of the main light on.

2
The Feather

There are only a few of them throughout the United Kingdom – a handful maybe, no more than six – and many others throughout the world at large. Beautiful angelic beings that, if not checked, their beauty would be out-marked by a devious… no, a majestic rivalry of evil, immense in proportion and opposing to any part of their light.

These beings are people: women and men who are only known to be what they embody by a mark, a symbol. That symbol is a feather. A beautiful feather of many colours tattooed down their spine, from the middle of their shoulder blades, about eight centimetres long, travelling vertically. The most beautiful image, if ever there was one: intricate, delicate, perfect, glowing very rarely. When it did, it illuminated from within the body. And the colours came from within, the tones being not of this world. Their hue was brighter than any artist could recreate. Yes, the colour came from within and without.

The feather shimmered with iridescent light. Its hues were turquoise, a salad of orange, grapefruit pink, and raspberry, phthalo green, a cerulean and electric blue, violet, searing white, and the sunshine yellow of a summer's day.

These unfortunate souls have been marked by evil, but have the capacity to be the light, the knowledge, the healing, and the beauty; the rescuers of our world! They do not know what they possess, and they remember almost nothing of the circumstances in which they received the mark, only that they are reminded daily by the intrusion of their own mind and thoughts, demoralising their self-esteem. These dark, intrusive thoughts appear by their very nature as violent flashes of scenarios and dark words, and which they themselves are repulsed by and subjected to as they try to get on with their daily lives and search for the truth that they know is inside of them!

They have all the answers, and they can see the truth, but the intrusive banter of unnerving chatter invades and defers the underlying marvel of glory which is possible to be finally achieved, and yet is denied so easily and delayed for the time being. Instead... a step in the right direction, a little knowledge to keep the thirst and the occupant engaged, frustrating and tiring these beautiful people. Because from evil comes beauty, from dark comes light, by the very nature of a perfect mind which only knows that it wants the light to triumph and not the dark.

Then a time would come when the feather would become warm and start to glow. Sometimes the intense heat would make the sufferer wince but see their own planet from a dark, starry viewpoint, one most beautiful.

I am one of those people who had been marked by the feather, although for the first 23 years of my life I did not know exactly what this meant. I had inklings of something that was available to me, and I also knew that there was more to me than met the eye. But I never knew what life had in store for me. I never knew what lay ahead!

3

The Darkness

The ice was slush that had frozen hard, thin, and strong. It was so difficult to keep upright, and even wearing spikes I had to concentrate hard whilst walking. It was tiring, and it made walking an unnatural thought process, a stressful, anxious task in which the necessary was a chore. Most people were removed from the effort involved to deliver what they were used to, although there were occasionally appreciative people who thanked me for the effort they realised I'd had to make. Most folk stayed indoors for those three days when walking was difficult. I saw the occasional elderly person who braved the outdoors, and I admired their strength, or need of necessity, to leave the house for their basic needs. As I trudged along, I realised how miserable, disgruntled, agitated, and tired I felt, and the weather didn't help. I dislike winter.

It is becoming more and more difficult for me not to give in to the dark side of the feather and what it represents; to the intense black thoughts of evil that don't seem to come from the truth that I feel from within. It's becoming almost impossible to stop the darkness from spilling out from me, by word of mouth and action. The immense feelings that I am finding difficult to control have almost taken over me. Not until it's almost too late am I saved by a thought, or a feeling, or some words which rescue me and all concerned from almost certain disaster!

This seems to be a running theme throughout my life, and looking back I must have been like this as a child, even though I didn't understand at the time. It must be why I needed to spend quite a bit of time on my own, in my own space, to be able to deal with so much going on in my brain. I need to be alone to work out how to control the power that could take over if I were to let it. On occasions, it just spills out of me. It's something that I can't unload onto other people by talking it through, because it's too surreal and difficult to understand.

So instead, I try to deal with it in my own head, every single day, every single hour, and almost every single minute. When I am worn out with trying to control this darkness, it breaks through as an angry outburst or a self-loathing. Sometimes I feel pure desperation, like I just can't go on. I understand that this is not an option, so I continue to drag myself through the desperate times with only hope in my heart. However dim or minute this particle of hope gets, it is always there, and it is the only grasp I have on the reality of living a life in this world.

I had a lot of friends in my childhood, and to this very day we still meet up. But no-one ever knew what was going on in my mind, because I couldn't have described it even if I wanted to. The complexities of one's mind may never be understood, and I knew that no-one would have believed me. I felt very lonely at times, and often cried because I wanted to go home – even when I was at home! My mother was exasperated by this and just smacked me senseless, with the ferocity of someone who just didn't know what else to do! She was too tired from the working day to have a lot of patience. My arms, bottom, and tops of legs were red raw afterwards! Then I was sent to my room, where I went to bed and cried myself to sleep.

I still remember that feeling, as if I had been torn away from all that I loved and placed somewhere completely foreign to me, where I felt I didn't belong! I clearly recall those moments of pure heartache as a young child, when I was crying and couldn't stop! When my mum asked me what was wrong, I said that I wanted to go home. I remember that desperate, all-consuming feeling of being homesick and wanting to go home so much that it physically hurt! Was I supposed to be somewhere else?

'YOU ARE AT HOME!' Mum would shout. She used to become so annoyed when I cried.

At times I would read by the open fire, or just spend time alone in my room, which gave me great comfort. I started to feel so different to everyone else around me; it was intense, painful, unreal, complicated, and frustrating.

On one occasion, when I was just lying on my bed trying to understand my thoughts, my mum shrieked angrily, 'Johanna! Come down!' She always called me by my full name when I had irritated her in some way!

I ran downstairs, and Mum said that my friends were at the door. Damn! I was in the middle of something and wanted to be on my own, so I asked her to tell them that I was asleep. She did, but later on she told me off and said that was the last time she was going to lie for me!

It's funny how one remembers the little things even after the years roll by.

4
The Voice

Someone was coughing in a heavy-smoker-in-the-morning kind of way. It sounded like they were clearing their chest of the debris of years of lung abuse! It took a while before I could open my eyes. They felt too weighty to be able to just open them by simply thinking of opening them. No, this morning it required a lot more effort to be able to see my bedroom window and look out at the sky to take in what kind of day it was. It felt like I had experienced one of those dreams where I had learnt something of tremendous value and importance, that would stand me in great stead for the years to come and the way forward in my life. Sometimes I was able to remember clearly the details of my dreams, and on a rare occasion could read into the subtle symbols and revelatory situations which had occurred. But not today. Such a pity, because I knew that my unconscious mind had received some realisation of tremendous value!

Some are realisations of a powerful nature, but when looked at more closely, they are simple truths that I could understand before but in a different way... The problem with these constant realisations is that someone somewhere is always just ahead of you. No, strike that! A lot of people for centuries have always been there, or realised and experienced something or another before you! So, what is the point of having these realisations if they are already known, can be passed on to you through generations, or read in a book, or looked up online?

Actually, I understand now. The point is that whatever anyone passes on to you via information from a book, or word of mouth, or wisdom passed down over the years, it never really means anything or is never truly understood until one has experienced it for oneself! It would be easier if you could be told the wisdom from others, and feel it and know it, and learn from it there and then. But you have to experience anything to be able to understand it or believe it totally.

Once you have experienced it, only then can you understand something someone may have said to you years before! You can tell someone something until you're blue in the face, but it may not sink in until that person has experienced something similar themselves, or until they are ready for it. And even then, your version of experiencing something will never be the same as someone else's experience of a similar situation. However much you can empathise with anyone else and have gone through a similar circumstance, we are all different, and everything is relative.

There is always someone who thinks that their pain is worse than that of others, but that is their selfishness. People say it's human nature, but is it? That is why one can never judge another human being, whatever the circumstance. How on earth can one person judge another when they cannot possibly know what the other is really going through, however similar or worse a situation they have experienced themselves?

Hindsight is a permanent experience for me! I may be slower to catch on to things than most, though not as slow as others, but I am what I am! I do not pretend to understand more than anyone else, nor be more intelligent than anyone else, either intellectually or emotionally. I can only relay my own experiences, and maybe someone somewhere could be comforted in the knowledge that they are not alone. Like anything in life. The complexity of a human mind is, of course, immense, and we are only able to use parts of this at a time. Even then, it seems to get the better of me! One of the emotions I often feel is fear, but it disguises itself as different emotions so that I react badly.

Fear is an enemy of us all. Now, if I were to rid fear from my mind, then I would have limitless strength, health, happiness, and wisdom! There would be far more possibilities made available to me, and I would be able to tap into creativeness with greater ease, and be in the fortunate position of having an abundance of positivity!

The saying goes: 'There is nothing to fear but fear itself.' I never understood this until recently, but I now find myself saying it over and over in my mind to keep me going.

Enough procrastination, I told myself, *it's time you were up!*

Only a strong cup of coffee was going to make my body and mind able to function this morning! Maybe it was because I had a day off that I had slept so heavily, knowing that I didn't have to get up early. The coughing had stopped now, and I realised it was Scott, one of my neighbours who coughed on the two-metre journey from his front door to his works van every morning.

I got out of bed, dressed, and clumsily made my way down the steep staircase, through the living room, and into the kitchen. Tilly must have been bored of waiting, as she scuttled in from the front room and stood by the cat flap waiting for me to let her out for a quick wee. She didn't go far in the mornings until she'd had her breakfast and a good look out of all the windows to see if there were foxes to chase, or her arch enemy 'Pirate' to watch out for.

One-and-three-quarters of a teaspoon of coffee with semi-skimmed milk. I took the coffee back upstairs to finish while I was getting dressed. It tasted good, and I started to feel better.

Another day, another dollar... Or another pound, another round. Not today! Today was my day off. Yay!

What to wear, though? It was always a conundrum. I didn't have a great deal of clothes, but there were enough to be able to choose from. It was quite mild today for the end of February, but a bit dreary looking as I peered through the bathroom window.

I opened my wardrobe by flipping up the material door with matching lavender bags hanging from each loop. I had two wardrobes: one for bottoms, and one for tops – both with the clothes arranged in colour sections. I decided on some French navy linen trousers and a blue, sage green, and raspberry stripy top with three-quarter length sleeves. I put an under-top on just in case a chill became apparent, and my new wedge-heeled burgundy boots, which were incredibly comfortable.

I got my taste in clothes in general from my mum and her sister, not that you would have known it when I was younger. We hadn't much money, but they both had good taste, which was either hippy or a version of the fashion of the time, whereas I plumped for cheap, tacky, and sometimes lurid options. When we went shopping, they were good enough not to dissuade me from getting the clothes I chose. Maybe it was because it was only once a year at Whitsun that we had a new outfit, but I was too excited to realise that they were repulsed by my choice. As I grew up, I noticed the furtive looks they exchanged, but my taste had taken root by then, and so I went with it.

Nowadays, I have quite a conservative taste, but with a twist of quirkiness. In fact, I think to the onlooker I might appear to be something that I am not – until I open my mouth, that is! The twang of my home town – and the rough side at that – usually bursts out without me really thinking about what I am saying. I can converse with the best and the worst, and feel at home anywhere or in any situation I find myself in. Maybe it's because I am mostly oblivious to others' reaction to me. There are no airs and graces with me. I am what I am, and my accent is as strong as it always has been. However, I do sometimes notice on certain days or at certain periods of time, that people have a bizarre reaction towards me. Sometimes they can seem quite aggressive, extremely defensive, do a double take when they look at me, or look me up and down in a puzzled way! But I can never work out why. At other times, people show a warmness towards me, as if I am perfection itself, which I don't understand either.

I left the house with a spring in my step, looking forward to seeing Lisa and the kids. She lived out in the sticks, and it would take about 25 to 30 minutes to get to her house; less, if the roads were quiet. Lisa was a good friend that I had met at work. We always have a laugh together, as she has a wry sense of humour and is always joking around. She was currently on maternity leave with a new baby, and already had a six-year-old boy.

The mid-morning traffic wasn't too bad, but there were lots of traffic lights and speed cameras on this journey. I was concentrating on keeping my speed down from 40 to 30 when I thought I saw a dead or injured dog lying in the middle of the road. I slowed down, and as I approached the scene, I felt the fear that I so often experienced when my thoughts rushed too far ahead with possible scenarios that could occur. Then it became clear that it was some packaging that lay in a crumpled heap and had been crushed by vehicles. No doubt it had fallen of the back of a lorry or blown from someone's recycling.

Unfortunately, I never seem to feel the relief that one should experience when fear and sadness are blown away to reveal a happy outcome. Instead, I feel the frustration of experiencing the atrocity of the pain and suffering that could have been. Maybe it's because this sort of thing has been happening so often.

Lately, I had begun to receive thoughts of an unchartered nature, by which I mean that I didn't know where they come from. As the weeks have come and gone, I have been feeling more and more exasperated by these thoughts.

As I continued to drive over the hill and descend towards the large roundabout to take the bypass, it came upon me like a flash that this was not a new experience for me. Of course! I had always had… 'The Voice'!

It's just that lately I had become more able to distinguish The Voice from my other, more acceptable thoughts, which I assume other people have. The Voice had become distinct from the other thoughts and not something that I had been accepting as the norm. As well as The Voice, I also had disturbing images. The dialect and the image almost invariably came together, but were sometimes separate.

Then there were times when I was in the moment, which felt great! A clear lake, pebbles on a beach, bird song, the smell of flowers, an animal's innocence, the wind in the trees – only to be coarsely interrupted by a thought popping into my mind!

Bam! The Voice!

**

I call it 'The Voice', and I tell it off all the time! Is it negative chatter of my own? No, it isn't; or it doesn't seem like it, anyway. Negative chatter occurs a lot, of course, in my own mind, probably as it does in everyone else's, but I do seem to have an excess of this stuff. This depressing, anxious, endless chatter which drives me insane at times! It is usually when I am concerned about a person, a situation, an animal, a future or past worry, which (if I'm up to it) I can usually blast with positive particles, or stop myself from thinking negatively.

No, The Voice is a thought in my own mind, in my own thought voice... I think, anyway. I encourage myself not to worry so much, that everything will be ok, and I tell myself off endlessly about thinking like this, constantly contradicting my own thoughts. It's a tiring existence, I can tell you!

So, then, whose voice is it? It sounds like my thought voice, but comes completely out of the blue, randomly, when I'm not thinking or worrying about the subject that it pertains to, that it is conveying to me, or the person that it is talking about! This is a voice that seems to have no connection to me at all. It's dark, it's negative, violent, and gruesome. I can be going about my daily business, down the shops, on the high street, at work, waiting at the dentist, waiting for a bus, not waiting for a bus, driving – in fact, at any time and in any place. It has even had the unprecedented audacity to pop in whilst I am trying to meditate! At a time which should be of pure joy, of being in the moment, of experiencing happiness in its purest form! How about them apples!

The Voice can talk about people that I love, people I don't know, and situations that are so upsetting that I don't wish to have them in my own mind. It's gruesome and dark, to say the least. It seems to be not of me. It invades me, and my space, and my mind. I do not wish to listen to it. I find myself telling it to stop, go away, and even swearing at it. I tell it that I want absolutely nothing to do with it. What or who is it? I need to find out. I have had it all my life.

My earliest experience of The Voice that I can recall is when I was about seven or eight. (Maybe younger, it's difficult to know.) I was in the back garden, which was very small – a back yard, really – but to me then it seemed ample enough space for a swing and a see-saw, a coal shed, and an area for plants and flowers.

I was playing, and my dad was busy working away. There I was, trying to pluck up the courage to talk to my dad about The Voice, which was difficult because even then I was a moody, quiet child at times, and used to keeping these thoughts and The Voice to myself. I remember being particularly upset at the time, because The Voice – or thought that had recently invaded my mind – was its usual gruesome image of someone close to me, who I love dearly, dying in a rather unsightly fashion. I think the thought was of my dad dramatically being killed somehow. If I remember correctly, it involved a beheading of some sort!

So, there I was in the garden, my dad planting in the soil edge of the paved back yard, when I just burst out and made it known to him that I was experiencing very disturbing thoughts. (Obviously in eight-year-old words.) He was suitably concerned, but told me not to worry and to just ignore it, so I did, and have tried to ever since.

I arrived at Lisa's house more tired than I should have been after a thirty-minute journey. I let myself in as usual, because Lisa was always somewhere in the house, changing a nappy, or feeding the baby, or looking for an item of clothing. I called out. Chase barked, but always gave me a lovely greeting by jumping up and looking softly and lovingly into my eyes. It turned out Lisa was in the kitchen feeding the baby.

We hugged and she gave me a concerned look, her brow wrinkled as she asked, 'Are you ok?'

'Yes,' I said, feeling slight embarrassment that I must look as tired as I felt. 'I'm just tired.'

'Yes, you've had a busy time of it lately, haven't you?'

'Yeah, but I am looking forward to a relaxing day off.'

As Lisa passed me the baby, I realised how much she had grown; she weighed a ton! Chase sloped up to me, knowing that at any minute he would be chastised by his owner for being a nuisance. On this occasion, he got away with it, as Lisa was busy preparing the baby's bottles for the day ahead, so he promptly flopped down onto my feet. I was encased in the weight and love from a baby and a dog. It felt good.

There are only a handful of people in my life I can rely on. The ones that I don't see for a while, but yet I can pick up with them and enjoy a life-changing time together. Those friends who you can forget the world with.

'Let's go for a long walk. I need to shift some of this baby weight. I feel like a fucking womble,' said Lisa.

5

The Passenger

The problem with having a day off, I find, is the wrench of going back to work the next day. But I felt suitably refreshed after spending time with Lisa and the kids.

Once I am up, it literally takes me seconds to get ready. I don't bother with makeup for work. There's no point, as the outdoor elements would soon obliterate any lipstick, eyeliner, or mascara. Without it, at least I can be sure that I look roughly the same starting off as finishing the day.

It was a dark, cold morning in February, and it was just before six am when I pulled up in Frank Street in my usual Saturday parking space – a ritual which had suitably disgruntled a resident of the street enough to have previously left a note on my car windscreen. My place of work was just through the trees, along the short pathway to the main road, but all the parking spaces were taken up by the local residents the evening before, and by my work colleagues who started even earlier than me.

Saturday mornings were not my favourite. Instead of getting to work for seven-thirty am, I had to set my alarm for five am, and get in for six! I am not a morning person, and it takes a good couple of hours and a fair amount of caffeine for me to come round.

Everyone in the small, dark, dead-end street was still asleep. It felt like all the other mornings when I would park the car and make a short hop through the bushes, quickly making sure that there was no-one hiding there.

Before getting out of the car, I looked in my rear-view mirror to check that I was not parked too close to the one behind…

'Shit!' I gasped.

THERE WAS SOMEONE SITTING IN THE BACK SEAT OF MY CAR!

A short intake of breath, a quiet gasp, and for a few seconds my breath was suspended before I realised that I needed to breathe!

I sensed it was a male.

I didn't scream, wet myself, or get out of the car and run.

Instead of feeling heart-wrenching, gruelling fear to the pit of my stomach, to my absolute amazement, I felt… pure joy!

A blissful feeling flooded throughout every vein in my body, like I had received an injection of some sort, and the material that had been injected into me was flowing fast and reaching every single cell of me.

You might think that I would be suitably startled to see someone whom I hadn't invited into my car, suddenly appear, sitting calmly on the back seat. But no, I was not startled in the conventional sense!

There seemed to be no time for the inevitable questions of who, what, and why. Instead, I felt pure love and wanted this feeling to last for eternity. There was no other moment as important as this, and there were no other thoughts other than this moment. I felt a release, as if I didn't have any weight to me, like I was not of me.

It's hard to describe the image I saw which, by the way, was still there for a good few seconds when I turned round to face him! He was, I would say, 75 percent solid. I could see through him, but at the same time he was three-dimensional. The huge figure was almost translucent. He reminded me of a Pablo Picasso portrait during his abstract period. The portrait of Wilhelm Uhde is the closest I can describe or compare him to. There was a solidity to him, but all his facets were of a transparent, jelly-like substance. I remember clearly seeing all the angular shapes that made his solid frame, but I could sort of see inside him and through him.

I was thankful. I was amazed. I felt pure joy and love. Then complete satisfaction and calmness of mind and body. We felt connected. I knew he was a friend and here to help me. He was beautiful, wise, sent from God…

I am not sure how long I sat in the car. It seemed like there was no time, that time never existed. But eventually, the figure sitting on the back seat disappeared as quickly as he had come, and I must have realised that I had to get to work.

As I walked, I felt a warm glow down my back and realised it was emanating from the feather. I felt the colours and the detailed barbs of the feather being etched even deeper into my skin, my very being! I knew that I was being prepared somehow for the work that I was meant to do, and that this was another step in the right direction.

When I arrived at work, I received a few quizzical looks. I felt flushed, and I realised that I was grinning from ear to ear. It was difficult to prevent myself from laughing out loud, but if I did, I would have had to explain why!

I don't know how I managed to get through that Saturday at work, because to say my concentration was poor that morning would be a huge understatement. My mind was on my new acquaintance and what I had experienced earlier. Was he a hallucination? A figment of my imagination? Was I losing it? Going mad? Did I need to tell someone?

I decided no. It was *my* experience, and I didn't want to denigrate it by letting someone else's disbelief and astonishment make a mockery of it all.

6

Time Travel

After yesterday's elation of meeting the passenger, I felt a bit deflated when I woke up and had to do the daily chores – washing up, putting a load in the washing machine, going to the supermarket, hoovering round, etc. It feels like it's a waste of my energy, my time, and my life to have to keep the environment around me clean and free from germs, but it has to be done! All the while I was thinking that I should be doing something else and trying to get it all finished as quickly as possible, but it seemed that as soon as one task was finished, I noticed another that needed doing.

There is always an endless amount of cleaning, tidying, and sorting, if you look for it. And one could spend their entire life doing these chores, until they are either too old or dead!

I needed to get out of the house and take a break from this, otherwise I felt that I might end up in an exhausted heap, with a cloth in one hand and a bottle of AntiBac in the other! I decided to go for a cycle, just local, and maybe pop into a few shops. I needed to get some presents for a few birthdays which were coming up.

I got my bike from the alleyway and pumped the tyres to almost bursting. Then I picked up my rucksack and cycle helmet, and left as quickly as I could, in case the phone rang or I noticed that something else needed sorting. I felt a kind of excitement, as if this was a task that I wasn't used to doing. It was like I wasn't used to being a human, and to go out on this vehicle called a bike was an adventure.

What an odd feeling! My feather felt so alive, and I could sense small electric shocks throughout my body.

The enjoyment of cycling and moving my limbs felt amazing, and I enjoyed pottering around the shops as the mood took me. Usually, I am the type of shopper who has a list and goes in, gets what I want, then moves on to the next item on the list, with no messing – especially with a weekly food shop in one of the supermarkets. Whereas, if my friend Janet came along, we could take hours! She would walk slowly along each aisle, perusing almost every item.

Once, when we went Christmas shopping together, we separated to visit different department stores, and arranged to meet at a bench outside her chosen shop. I was sitting there for a whole hour, and refused to go in and look for her, knowing that if I did I would be embroiled into the shop. I was just about to give up and go and drag her out, when she appeared, accompanied by a security guard, carrying her bags for her! She staggered by the side of the hefty guard, high heels tottering, carrying so many bags that her small frame was almost hidden from view!

Today, though, I was enjoying looking round some of the independent shops in my area for gifts. Some people were so easy to shop for, like me. Then others were almost impossible, either because they were a certain age, or because they were fussy. I never know what to get for my mum, as she basically has everything she needs or doesn't need.

After a while, my small rucksack was bursting and becoming rather heavy, as I had bought a few bathroom essentials along the way. So, I decided to finish off and get back for a nice cuppa.

As I cycled home along the high street, I started to feel a bit odd again. It was a sort of excitement with a tinge of edginess; the kind you get when you are somewhere new and have a tingling feeling in your stomach. I shivered as the goosebumps spread up my arms and down my legs. I looked around and felt the atmosphere change, at the same time encompassing me.

It all seemed different somehow. As if I was in a different place. The shops seemed unfamiliar, as did the people and the air around me. The city-village boundary seemed to grow on every side. My surroundings expanded, and so did the invisible safety net of my community. This, I realised, was something I had taken for granted. The border of familiarity of the area in which I live and feel safe in, stretched unlimited beyond physical view. But now, it felt like I was in a different city. Manchester maybe? I have been there a few times, and this seemed reminiscent of a street in an area there.

Suddenly it came to me that I was still on the high street that I knew so well, yet somehow it all seemed so retro. I looked around. Was my mouth open? Check.

The shops seemed dated, and there was a little old lady standing outside a bakery. She was holding a large loaf of bread wrapped in greaseproof paper. She smiled and waved at me. I waved back, and even thought she seemed familiar to me, but I had no idea who she was. I must have looked like I had just been beamed down from another planet, but if my face showed the astonishment that I felt inside, she didn't seem to notice, and carried on walking slowly up the street. Another strange feeling came over me, an otherworldly one.

'What on earth?' I heard myself saying out loud.

'You alright, miss?' someone shouted.

I realised that I was no longer cycling along the road, but had come to a stop by a lamppost, which I was clutching rather tightly. I looked to my left, and standing on the pavement dressed in what looked like scruffy work garments, was a young man in his twenties.

'You alright, miss?' he repeated.

'Y-y-yes, I think so,' I replied in an unusual tone. 'Just felt a bit dizzy,' I heard myself say.

'Perhaps you had better push your bike the rest of the way,' said the smiling, mature sounding young man. 'Why don't you pop into the coffee diner for a cuppa till you feels betta?'

'Yes, thank you,' I said. 'That's a good idea.'

Coffee diner? I wondered.

He smiled and waved his hand as he carried on up the high street, and I waited till he had gone from view then quickly mounted my bike and headed for home.

'Oh God, I hope it's still there!' I found myself muttering.

As I cycled more slowly now, to take in my surroundings, I looked across to the right-hand side of the small high street and saw that the wholesale warehouse, which sold random bits and bobs, was missing. In its place were two large houses, with what looked like an old stable attached. Further up, as I cycled closer to my road, I noticed that the warden-controlled housing unit which used to be adjacent to the warehouse was no more. In its place was a beautiful old brick wall, a boundary to a wild flower wasteland area.

I stopped by the wall to ponder at the beauty and smell of the colourful scene before me. I could have stayed there enjoying the sunshine for much longer, but was worried about being able to get home. I felt a new all-consuming urgency to see my own front door.

I continued onwards towards my house, now feeling a great sense of panic. I realised that I was crying miserably. As I got closer to my house, I began to feel a little more like my old self again. But then something happened that made me forget all about these confused feelings.

I got ready to dismount my bike not far from the corner of the street, where the little shop ended and the pavement dropped. I cycled onto the pavement, up towards my front door – number 33. It is white PVC – not a colour or material I would have chosen, but it's a safe, strong door, so I can't complain.

Suddenly, something crossed my path and got in my way. What was it? There was a flash of colour, then a scream pierced my eardrums. In a moment of confusion, I turned my head and looked across to the other side of the street, and saw people running out of number 28.

At that time, number 28 was occupied by a sex worker called Dawn. She was a lively character who had been banned from the high street for stealing in most of the shops. I often saw her standing on the corner of the road waiting to be picked up by a car or a taxi. I don't think the halfway house rules would have allowed the customers to come to her!

She often asked me or the neighbours if she could use our mobile phone, but whenever she asked me, I flatly said no. I have a thing about germs and other people touching things that might have to go close to my face. Even when I use my mobile myself, I put it on speaker phone because I feel it is far more hygienic. There is also the fact that I can't speak on it for more than a couple of minutes without the side of my face burning or my ear heating up.

Then there was the time when Dawn knocked on my door, asking to borrow some foil. I asked her, 'What for?'

'I'm making brownies,' she replied innocently.

She didn't look like the baking type. I told her I had run out.

Now, Dawn was shouting at another woman, and there was a group of young men laughing and goading this woman, who was brandishing a large, sharp looking cake knife in her hand. A few of the neighbours started to pop out from their houses, here and there, wondering what was going on.

Trudy was on the corner in her dressing gown, although it was around five pm. It was a rather grubby looking, ragged thing with a variety of stains. She seemed to wear it as an overcoat in addition to her everyday clothes, whatever the weather. She said she felt warm and cosy in it.

Outside the corner house, there was a pile of bricks which had been left by a workman the previous day, and the knife-carrying woman started to pick up bricks in her free hand and throw them randomly around at the lads, missing her targets by a mile. Needless to say, there were a few choice landings on parked cars.

Someone shouted, 'I have dialled 999!' But there was no sign of the police.

A panicked thought occurred to me! I had better stand on the corner and see if my friend Janet was on her way round, as she had said she would pop by after work. And she was due any minute.

Braving the chaos, I just marched through, keeping a keen eye on where the crazed woman was heading. By the time I got to the corner of the road, she had run back into number 28. The lads soon disappeared, and the street became calm once more, with just a few of the neighbours gathered to discuss what had happened.

A few minutes later, sirens could be heard coming from the high street and, like a group of meerkats, the neighbours turned their heads in unison towards the now approaching police car. It screeched to a halt at the junction of Silver Birch Lane, and a young policeman almost fell in his rush to get out of the car. He breathlessly asked what had happened. He looked panicked and sweaty, and he was on his own.

'It's too late, she's gone now!' The Godfather shouted irritably.

I heard the policeman apologizing for his lateness and explaining that he had been forced to rush from another job a few miles away, but had got here as quickly as he could. The Godfather was not impressed, but I felt a little bit sorry for the young policeman.

I walked over to the corner again where Trudy was standing in her dressing gown, looking non-plussed.

'What happened?' I asked.

Trudy seemed to know most of the goings-on in the street, because she spent so much time outside her front door or someone else's. I often saw her loitering around the doors and windows of the neighbours, cadging Wi-Fi to use on her tablet. So, if anyone would know what had happened as I'd turned the corner from Silver Birch Road to Blossom Street, it would be her. And she did.

She embarked on the tale with gusto, in a very loud voice. It turned out that the crazed woman was the sex worker's sister, who had visited for the day. One of the lads was her sister's boyfriend, whom she had argued with. The other lads were her boyfriend's friends.

We chatted for a while, then it started to rain. As I walked to my door, I noticed most of the residents who had witnessed the event were now popping back into their houses one by one, except for The Godfather.

He stood staring at the policeman, who was still on the corner.

7

'The Godfather'

I woke up feeling somewhat drained from the working week. There had been various sales which were unusual for the time of year, with silly names that many retailers collaborated on to call 'Midnight Madness' or 'wall-to-wall sale', similar to the pre-Christmas events called 'Black Friday' or 'Cyber Monday'. So the parcel volume was way up.

Last night I decided that I had better do some online shopping, seeing as I was too busy delivering everyone else's goods to physically go shopping myself. Both my kettle and my toaster needed replacing. Although I've always preferred to browse the shops, I didn't mind purchasing these items online. The previous lockdowns were starting to finally become a memory of an earlier time, but there were still certain constrictions in place and habits left over from the pandemic. Even now I had a bad taste in my mouth from the queuing, and the inevitable unmasked shopper lunging too close or reaching over me, their body and face well within the prescribed two-metre distance rule! Those had certainly been dark times for this world...

For me, it seemed like I had woken up one day and the world was different, but I don't think anyone saw it coming in such a catastrophic way as it did. I used to wonder what to do. Was it too late to think positively? Was it too late to do all the things that I wanted to do, needed to do? Should I take the sensible approach or should I not? All that was left was love. That's all there has ever been, but people did not want to know about that. People wanted money and power. They were greedy and selfish and didn't do the right thing for our planet and its inhabitants. Young Greta had spoken, but still a lot of people didn't listen, because they were too selfish to think outside of their avaricious needs. I really needed to dig deep.

It rained and rained and rained... endless days turned into weeks of squelching around for hours, feeling uncomfortably wet. The floods came and went, and an elderly man died. There were 90-mile-an-hour winds, the lungs of our planet were uprooted. Then there was fire and disease. The world didn't feel safe any more. It seemed like I felt unclean, the world wasn't clean, and the glimpse of hope eternal had faded somewhat. The signs had been there all along, but not enough of us had taken enough notice, and then we found ourselves in the midst of despair and people were dying all around us!

Even in the worst of times there is always hope, I thought to myself. Of course, there is always hope. But is there hope only when you can feel the glimmer of it in your heart? Where is the hope when you can't see the tiny pinpoint of light to snatch before it escapes? Is there only hope when the despair is not total? Is hope relative, or is it always there regardless of the degree of desperation you feel?

This week had been rough on my body, but still I needed to stretch my limbs, and the sun was shining. After a coffee, a tea, and another coffee, I felt adequately fortified to be able to venture out to the shops to get some food in. I was down to my last toilet roll and no milk, so I gathered the belongings needed for a shopping trip and glanced outside the window as I picked up my keys.

'For goodness' sake!' I found myself saying out loud.

Don had blocked another unsuspecting car owner in! Don – Donald, known by the street as The Godfather – has a disabled parking spot, which he is fiercely protective of. So protective, in fact, that if anyone parks too close to the outer edges of the lines marked out by the council, he blocks them in either by parking so close that his bumper hits their car, or by parking parallel to them, ensuring that they know they have done wrong! Depending on where the surrounding vehicles are situated, this can result in the perpetrator not being able to leave the clutches of Blossom Road for quite some time.

Many an unsuspecting shopper, who parks in our road to walk the three minutes to the high street, has not realised the consequences of his or her actions – particularly if they have neglected to leave a sufficient distance to allow for the over-hang (the bit of the car from the wheel to the boot, and from the wheel to the front of the bonnet). Or not left enough of a gap after that, for easement of leaving the car parking space.

This can result in the unswerving wrath of a very angry pensioner, sometimes armed with a walking stick or, on certain days, with a golf club (not of the putting variety!).

The Godfather was in his eighties, but still a giant of a man. The years had not shrunk his stature at all. No stooping down with age for him. No-one had told him he was getting older. His faded tattooed arms from his rum-drinking navy days were always demonstrative of his words as he pointed or waved at passers-by.

He once showed me a list of car registration number plates in neat array. I wish that I had not asked what they were, as the answer had made me a possible accomplice to a potential crime. The list comprised any car that had parked in the street, including the regulars who lived there and anyone else who had ever had the audacity to park on our little road.

Visitors to our homes had to be made aware of the parking restrictions for their own wellbeing and protection. And any new person or family who moved into our road was soon put in their place by The Godfather, unless they were gently advised by me or another neighbour about the parking rules of the street.

He did have a good side to him, though –he would help anyone that he liked, who was in need. He was always there if I needed a hand with anything in the garden or some advice on a street issue. And I, or another neighbour, would usually be around to help the person who had been disturbed by his wrath. My neighbours all felt sorry that I had to live next door to him, but there were good and bad sides to everyone, and I just accepted who he was.

On the days when I have the misfortune to be leaving or entering my house, and when my car is parked on the other side of the felon when this scene is happening, Don hints to me that I should move my car bumper-to-bumper with said car, totally blocking in the poor shopper's vehicle. To this day, I have refused to be a part of this rigmarole by either pretending to be in a rush or acting dumb, but I am quickly running out of excuses. And unfortunately, I think that there will come a time when I have no choice other than be roped into this charade or suffer the consequences of The Godfather of our street.

This was one of those occasions, so I peeped through the blinds to see if it was all-clear. I didn't have time to listen to one of Don's grievances with another car owner. The Godfather always threatened to call the police, and on a few occasions they came. Had he some sort of arrangement with them? Were they in his pocket?

It seemed all-clear for the time being, so I ventured out and quickly made it to the corner of Blossom Road where I turned the corner into Stonecrop Street and was safe to get on with my day.

I was concerned that the other day's events (my unnerving adventures through the high street) would happen again, but this time everything went smoothly.

On returning home, I was witness to The Godfather telling the new neighbours that their garden was becoming too untidy for his liking. I felt embarrassed for them and rushed to the safety of my home before he tried to get me involved.

8

The Blood of Elsie

Best foot forward today, I told myself. I felt a vibration on the side of my leg and realised that my phone was ringing. I have never been able to work out how to get it to ring for longer, which invariably results in me missing my calls while I am fumbling about trying to get my phone out of my pocket. I often also forget to lock my phone, resulting in my friends and family receiving many pocket calls for the duration of up to four minutes. They can hear me walking along, banging gates, or the sound of my phone rubbing up and down on my leg.

I missed the call.

I glanced at the screen to make sure that it hadn't been my manager calling, then continued with my work. I was in a rhythm now, and it would be too disruptive to stop and ring the number back; I didn't have the time. As I turned the corner into New Road, I saw Elsie's partner walking down the road slightly ahead of me. He must have come out of 'that' house while I had my back turned. Thank goodness he was not stopping to say hello. Although I hadn't seen him for a little while, I had heard about his shenanigans from Elsie, who always rang when it got too much for her. If only she knew what I knew, or thought I knew!

Oh! He must have forgotten something, because he did a quick turn about and started walking towards me. I took a deep breath as he walked past without recognising me and carried on down the road. I kept my cap on down over my eyes. My relief was short-lived, though, when I heard what sounded like an aggressive shout. I wasn't sure what had been said, so I turned around. He seemed to be looking at me.

'Are you talking to me?' I said in a defensive, nasty kind of way. I knew I had a face on, because I felt my bottom jaw stick out uncomfortably. The feather stung.

He looked slightly taken aback and just muttered, 'Hello,' like someone who had been caught between a rock and a hard place. Who knows what was going on in his mind?

I have always found him to be much too intense to have a conversation with, so have kept my relationship with him to a bare minimum. I can only guess how frustrating it might be for him to see me, knowing that he is up to no good in front of his wife's good friend. I expect he thinks I report everything back to Elsie, but I don't, because that would cause too much trouble for all concerned. Best she found out the details herself. Elsie didn't need me to fill in the gaps. I am sure she had a pretty good idea of what he got up to – well, in the general sense, I suppose.

This man is so paranoid that I wouldn't be surprised if he thought I deliberately walked up and down the street where his misdemeanours were out for all to see. Just then, I realised that he had been calling the other woman's daughter who was walking towards us, but he had been forced to say hello to me.

Elsie had asked me if I knew where the other woman lived. I did know the precise house, but because of my job I could never have told her. I said I didn't know, but that I had bumped into him around the area she had referred to.

About a week ago, a work colleague had passed on a message to me from 'His Nibs' saying that I didn't do a very believable Irish accent, which confused me. I could only hazard a guess that someone had rung him up pretending to be someone else, using an Irish accent. He must have a high opinion of himself that he thinks I give a damn about what he does, says, and thinks, never mind be bothered to find his phone number and ring up pretending to be someone else. The idea was preposterous to me, and it made me so angry – but not for long. It wasn't worth my time. The truth couldn't be further away, but I must remember to ask for the exact details of the message.

I would be happy if I never had to bump into him again. I was tired of having to put up with him all these years, appearing at windows, following Elsie and me to see what was going on. I think he must be one of the most paranoid people that I have ever met.

There was one time that I had a birthday party – a big year for me – and the celebrations were in full swing, mostly in the garden. I went into the kitchen to wash some glasses and looked up from the sink to see 'His Nibs' staring through the window at me. He hadn't been invited, but he couldn't bear the thought of Elsie enjoying herself with other people – especially men.

Another time, I was approaching my house and said hello to The Godfather, who was at his door – the prime position. He kept a very close eye on the comings and goings of the street. I passed the alleyway which runs down the side of my house, and lo and behold, 'His Nibs' was skulking there. He was shocked that I had caught him out. I tried to act as if it was usual for someone to be skulking down said alley, and he tried to look like it was a normal thing to be lurking there. But Elsie wasn't even with me, nor had I seen her that day!

My phone rang again. It was a new phone which had a different ringtone that I wasn't accustomed to, so I looked around to see where the noise was coming from before I realised it was mine. I fumbled to answer it.

It was Elsie!

'Hello?' I felt flustered.

'I have done something stupid and am in the hospital. Can you pick me up later on when they have finished with me?' she said.

I felt a slight panic. As the feather fluttered, a sickly feeling came over me.

Breathe, I told myself.

'What have you done?'

'I've cut my hand open, and the doctor is doing some tests before he sews it back up,' Elsie replied.

'Well, I've nearly finished, so I could be with you in an hour,' I offered.

'Thanks,' she said, and she hung up.

I was concerned; Elsie didn't sound good at all. She sounded strange, but I suppose anyone would if they'd had an accident.

I finished work and drove straight to the hospital, found a parking space quite easily, and made a quick hop to the reception to see where she was.

A nurse directed me to Accident and Emergency. I was shown to the desk and, while waiting for someone to be available to ask where Elsie was, I noticed a lot of blood on the floor leading to a cubicle with a splashed, blood-stained curtain. I must have outwardly winced, and a nurse caught my eye.

I blurted out, 'That's not my friend Elsie's blood, is it?'

A couple of the nurses exchanged furtive looks.

'Come this way,' one of them said.

I could hear my heart beating outside of my chest; it was loud, and I felt sick and dizzy. I followed the nurse, and could feel the displeasure of it all written on my face as I was shown into the cubicle by way of the bloody trail. The curtain was pulled aside for me, thankfully, as I wouldn't have wanted to touch anything, and there was Elsie with her hand bandaged up, looking sheepish. I was relieved to see she was sitting up and talking.

'What happened?' I asked as I hugged her gently, avoiding her left-hand side.

She told me that she had tried to lift up the big sash window in her living room, when the glass had dropped out and badly sliced her hand! I wasn't convinced, because I couldn't work out in my mind how that could have happened, but I didn't say anything.

We waited for the doctor to come and test her hand to see if the movement had been affected. Elsie told me that a very nice man had already been in to clean the wound and have a look. He had explained to her that he needed to get the surgeon to examine her hand thoroughly, and that it shouldn't take too long, as she was first on the list after Dr Jawad's lunch break.

Then Elsie went on to tell me that 'His Nibs' had been hounding her, following her, waiting on corners, driving by, and accusing her of seeing other men. Generally acting crazy. He had also been letting himself into her house when she wasn't there, as she had noticed that things had been moved, and he had left his phone on one occasion. He was certainly one of the oddest behaving men I had ever come across. Thank God he couldn't get into my house, because I am sure he would want to. *Had he tried*? I wondered. *Those times when I've caught him skulking, waiting to see if Elsie was up to something she shouldn't be?* The reason I had always acted like it was normal to find him skulking around was because I was so used to it. And I was concerned that if I behaved like it wasn't normal, it might bring about an adverse reaction from him. He was not a man to offend or contradict, because the consequences could be serious, depending on his mood, which was always very stern, defensive, and dodgy.

Elsie seemed unhinged, and I caught two of the nurses looking over and whispering to each other. *Had she behaved in a difficult manner?* I wondered. There was definitely a sense of something untoward in the atmosphere. But she seemed calm, for the moment at least. While I waited with her, I felt an urge to ask exactly what had happened with the sash window, but I didn't want to irritate her any more than she already was. In this calmer state, she would be more manageable and agreeable when I drove her home, so I felt that it was best to leave things be.

The doctor eventually arrived as we were discussing what Elsie had been doing prior to the 'accident'. She said she had been cooking one of her favourite Jamaican dishes with dumplings. The room had been getting warm and steamy from the cooking, so she said that she had wanted to air the house by opening all the downstairs windows.

The doctor arrived with the surgeon just as Elsie was about to explain in more detail exactly what had occurred.

'I have my colleague with me who specialises in this type of hand injury, and he is going to do some tests before I stitch you back up,' the doctor said.

'So, Elsie, is it?' asked the surgeon. 'I'm Dr Jawad. What on earth have you been up to?'

He had a laid-back manner about him, as well as being handsome, cool, calm, and collected. I exchanged a raised eyebrow with Elsie; we could both appreciate a handsome doctor.

Dr Jawad looked at the wound with some sort of magnifying instrument, while Elsie turned away to look at me, and I averted my gaze away from her hand to look at her. We both looked thoroughly disgusted, and on seeing each other's expressions, started to giggle.

'Ok,' the surgeon said, 'I can't see a foreign object in there; it looks pretty clear to me. Dr Jenkins has done a good job in cleaning this wound for you. Right, Elsie, I am going to do some preliminary tests for movement.'

As Elsie followed his directions, I saw her wince with pain, and a small amount of blood spurted out of the wound when she was asked to do a particular movement. I looked away, grimacing.

'Whoa!' said Dr Jawad, and gently wiped Elsie's hand with the care of a parent wiping a baby's bottom.

'Hmmm.' He turned to address the other doctor, who had been observing. 'Have a look at this.'

'Oh!' Dr Jenkins said. 'It looks like you're a very fast healer, Elsie. Your tendon is already knitting back.' They both looked at each other with puzzled expressions, and Dr Jawad frowned at Dr Jenkins as if to question why he had called him there.

Dr Jenkins looked into the wound and with a baffled expression he began stitching her hand.

At that moment, The Voice piped up: *'You think you're so clever!'*

I just ignored it.

I decided this was not the time to mention having seen 'His Nibs' earlier in the day, but the irony and absurdity of the situation hit me as I took Elsie's arm and escorted her out of the hospital to my car. I drove her home and made her a cup of tea.

Luckily, it was a very short trip to where she lived.

9
The Day After

'Enough with your procrastination. I need to be doing whatever it is that I need to be doing!' I mumbled to myself.

I woke up today feeling drained again, and did not want to go to work. The feeling was all-consuming, and I found myself crying uncontrollably. *What the hell is wrong with me now? I* thought. *It's just going to be more stressful ringing in and making an excuse than just getting out of bed and going. I know I will feel better once I am up. I always do.* I told myself to get a grip.

The previous day's events were replaying over and over in my head as I gulped my coffee down. I started coughing uncontrollably. A small amount of liquid must have slipped down my gullet.

'Just get dressed for fuck's sake, you moron.'

'Shut the fuck up,' I said out loud.

What had Elsie done? Did I really want to know? I had left her curled up on a comfy chair with her cat, Igor. He was a huge blue tom cat, with a surly face, but he was soft when it came to Elsie. He regarded me with disdain, akin to a human who hated me so much they would spit in my face! She hadn't wanted to talk, so I had made her a drink and left.

This giving 100% all of the time was exhausting. There was no life in the feather at all today. It felt insipid, and so did I. I could see that I might get away with not giving 100% all the time, but what if I was a doctor? Like Dr Jawad? Would I have to give 100% all the time then? Whatever situation I am in, I can see from all viewpoints; it's like I am limitless, omnipotent, and omnipresent! I can see it from my side, from the side of the person I am dealing with, and from the points of view of the people all around me. But it can drain all my physical and mental energy away. Yesterday had worn me out; I even knew what the nurse was thinking at one point.

Although I wondered how Elsie was feeling this morning, I didn't dwell on it. *I'll ring her after work*, I thought. If she was up to it, I'd pop by for a cuppa.

There was no light inside me today, no glow, no colour – or if there was, I couldn't feel it. The feather sank inside my body and shrivelled up, like a crisp autumn leaf.

Work was a blur as I dragged myself around, delivering what I needed to with no joy. I forced a smile to be courteous when I had to interact with anyone, but that was it. I finished work feeling physically unwell. I had pain throughout my body, a slight headache, a sore throat, and no energy. Elsie hadn't answered her phone, so I decided to go straight home.

The Godfather was on his doorstep, checking out some number plates, notebook in hand.

'Hi Don,' I called.

He just looked at me inquisitively, with one eyebrow raised.

'I just need a sleep,' I said, as I let myself into my house.

Closing the door, I heard Don say, 'You always need a sleep.'

I slumped on my new comfy chair in the living room and put on some classical music. It made me cry. Only for a short time, though, then I felt better. I slept, then took a tablet.

My anxiety brought me this physical discomfort. I know that anxiety, stress, and negative thoughts result in dis-ease. Unfortunately, thought to reality can be instant with me! It always has been. I realise that there is poison in my body, which is stuff I haven't been able to talk about. I try to ignore the uncomfortable negative thoughts which come into my mind. I acknowledge them and ask them to leave. I try to think of my clear lake and it's beautiful...

What a waste of a day.

10
Running With It

It was a lovely Monday in early April. The sky was blue with a few cirrus clouds slicing through it. The sun was out, and the wind was cool. There were little neat piles of lambs' tails collected in the road and on the pavement. There was definitely something in the air today! It felt like summer holidays when I was young, even though it was coming up to Easter and there was still a chill in the air.

As I got into the car to go and visit Lisa, I felt good, although I was a little tired from the weekend I had spent in my home town. I always enjoyed the journey to see Lisa. It was the familiarity of the visit that I found comforting. Driving along today, though, I started to feel uncomfortable. Well, maybe that's too strong a word. It felt like something was wrong. My view seemed to switch and adjust as I drove. A touch of vertigo, perhaps? Looking through the wrong part of my varifocals?

Thinking I had better pull to the side of the kerb, I blinked a few times, took a few deep breaths, and indicated left. But it was too late. A car that I hadn't even noticed, was driving straight towards me. Closing my eyes, I braced myself for a head-on collision. I felt an electric current running through my body which made me quiver quite violently. It felt like someone had walked over my grave, or some unearthly soul had flown through me. Then I felt uplifted, powerful, and light. The feather fluttered. Everything was going to be ok. I had no worries, like nothing was as important as this feeling. I must be dead!

'Just open your eyes,' someone said clearly and authoritatively.

I obeyed the command and opened my eyes. Some people, cars, and buildings were not as clear as others. There seemed to be another world showing itself. I was still driving in the left-hand lane. These ambiguous objects and people were moving in a different direction to everything else! I panicked for a second or two, then realised that I could continue driving safely as long as I concentrated. I slowed down considerably. There seemed to be other people from a different place or time simultaneously living in the same space. It was all so familiar, but separate somehow.

I decided that I wasn't dead, and looked in my rear-view mirror to see where the other car had gone. There was nothing untoward, no smashed-up car, no devastation after a crash. A crowd hadn't formed. I puffed out my cheeks as I exhaled.

So, what was I seeing? I wasn't scared any more, and I didn't even feel uncomfortable. I could see these other people in this other place, but knew I was ok; it was safe. Was this going to be a regular occurrence where another place showed itself? It was a good feeling, and made me grin insanely. I gave thanks that I was able to see this.

From that first time, when I saw the passenger in the back of my car, this 'seeing' had built up gradually. The other day, when I pulled into the street coming back from work, I saw The Godfather talking to Scott. There was a woman I hadn't seen before standing by his side. She was pointing her finger at a car parked next to his, and looked disgruntled. She looked like she could have given The Godfather a run for his money! They made a good team.

Scott looked very uncomfortable, but as long as they had his attention, I reckoned I could slip into my house unnoticed. By the time I had parked and got out of the car, there was only The Godfather left at his doorstep, looking annoyed. I had wanted to stay in the car until they had all retreated into their homes, but The Godfather had seen me and waved, so that was no use. Scott had been slowly stepping back into his house while The Godfather rattled on.

I arrived at my door, hoping he wouldn't keep me too long, as I was hungry and tired. But he proceeded to tell me the story of the couple who had the audacity to park outside his house and go shopping to the high street. I mean, they weren't in his disabled space, but had encroached on the line a couple of centimetres. I asked him who the woman was that had been standing next to him just now, and he looked at me like I was nuts!

'What woman?' he asked.

'Oh, it doesn't matter,' I muttered.

Another realisation suddenly came to me. I reckon this has been happening all my life, but I just haven't seen it as clearly. Lately, though, I have noticed more with my physical eyes – the people, animals, and the scenery from the 'other place'. But they have always been there by my side, and all around me; another world happening at the same time as the one we all see. Here and there, on the odd occasion, I have seen people as clear as day and much more frequently. I get a sense that it has taken a lot of preparation by someone – as well as me being ready and willing to understand – to be able to differentiate between here and there. I think I have started to interpret the various phases of this world and the next.

The feeling was getting stronger. Where was I supposed to be, or, more to the point, what was I supposed to be doing? It nags at me each day with a growing sense of urgency. I need to know before it's too late to do the work that I am supposed to be doing. I feel like my life has been leading up to something very important. This something is the only thing that I am meant to do. Everything in my life has been building up to this moment – one when I am supposed to know exactly what to do with my life. Every little thing, every experience, every job, every skill. Every person that I've met, every moment that I have had, is vital for the work I am meant for. Born for. For goodness' sake, please show me, let me know, God, please…

You know when it's time, and if you resist, then hopefully you will get another opportunity and take it. Perhaps you thought you were ready, but the time wasn't right. It's rare; perhaps fate, when you are blessed with the opportunity and also feel ready! I think I am ready now. All the factors have come together. Unfortunately, all my life things just seemed to simmer under the surface for such a long time before they would materialise or come to fruition.

Over the years I have looked up my horoscope to try and get an insight into my character outlined by the stars. It always says that Capricorns are: 'introverted and ambitious, but last to rise to the top, who sacrifice their own immediate gratification for long-term achievements. Like a mountain goat, they climb the greatest heights in solitude.'

It also says that there is a great disparity between the way I feel about certain situations and the impressions I offer to an unsuspecting world. There is a screen between the way I feel and the façade I show to the world at large.

When I am talking to someone, or more specifically trying to explain to a friend or colleague or anyone how I feel about something, or how I am going to take a particular task on, or any damn thing really, I can actually see by looking at their face that they are understanding what I am saying in a particular way. But it's not in the way that I am trying to portray ! I give up eventually. The light shows on their face when they retell what they have understood about our conversation, and I try my best to tell them that's not really what I meant. But it ends up being too difficult, because they don't understand. And then I get confused and I don't understand, so a lot of the time I just don't bother.

I can't wait any more, but what for I don't know. My overflow was full, and had started to overflow.

What's going on? Does anyone know what's really happening?

11
That Day

This was one of those days that you could never forget. One of those mind-blowing days, after which one is never the same again. And not just for me, but for my cousins, and probably for many more of the hundreds who were in attendance.

Today had been building up in my mind for a few weeks. I can usually block an event I am not looking forward to until the day it happens, so that I can get on with life without the extra mind stuff that builds up in the doleful anticipation of going to a funeral. Who wants all that mind mess swamping their brain and clouding their intellect?

I was determined not to let The Voice get a look-in. This, though, was going to be difficult for all concerned. I find it harrowing coping with other people's sorrow, much more than my own, and even more so when it comes to family.

I'd received a phone call about three weeks ago to say that my uncle had passed away. We were all expecting it, and I had travelled up the country to see him about a month before the phone call. He had asked me to choose something practical from a catalogue to remember him by. He was a very sincere man, and I loved him so much!

I couldn't remember getting up this morning or getting ready to go, or the journey up here to the place where my uncle had lived for a good part of his life. But here I was, with my aunty beside me. My parents were further forward in the pews, and one of my cousins to the rear. I was anxious. My cousin should be at the front near his mum and brother, but he was behind me. Why?

My uncle had arranged the funeral before he died. He had chosen the hymns and the readings, because he knew that it would all be ok in the end. He was watching the events as they unfolded before him, and understood before anyone else what the day would bring.

As I walked solemnly into the church in line with others, a man crossed my path. I didn't know him, but he looked at me as if he knew something about me that I did not. He looked into my eyes, put his hands together just below his chin, and bowed his head to greet me. That man, the one with the beautiful soul! The one wearing a burnt orange turban. He just looked into my soul and bowed his head. So I bowed mine back. His hand stretched out, and before I knew it, he had placed something into my palm and closed my hand tight. He knew! Much more than I did! He knew the answer!

Was this moment orchestrated to be? I felt a warm glow on my back and the heat started to become very intense very quickly. I felt excited, but was concerned that the light from the feather would be seen through my clothes. I realised this had never been an issue before, because the clothes I wore were usually of suitably substantial material. Today, the glow was dazzling enough for me to realise it was happening. Today, it felt noticeably different.

The heat had become so intense that I started to feel like I was about to self-combust. A memory from a programme I had watched about the seventies flooded my mind. I did not want to end up as a pile of ashes and a pair of shoes. As I was deciding whether to nip outside quickly for some air until the heat subsided, I noticed a few furtive and comforting looks came my way. I think I must have made a sound that I wasn't aware of. Eventually, I was able to rest back on the pew and take note of my surroundings. I didn't want to bring any more attention to myself because of the glow. *Why on earth had I picked this transparent top to wear today of all days?*

The song that was playing! 'He showed me where he was Atman that man I could not see.'

I went to a calm and peaceful place; one I had been to many times before. I was standing in front of the sea, and this time the tide was out. The old man was there. We had been looking at pebbles, which was our favourite pastime together. As I held the beautifully smooth sand and stone coloured pebble in my hand, I said, I wonder if that line penetrates all the way through the stone, or does it just cover the surface?

As he came to stand beside me, he replied in his gentle voice, 'It does go completely through the stone; it is akin to your spirit. It is not just cosmetic or shallow, it reaches from deep within, and as you can look into a person's eyes and read what is happening in their soul, so you can read this pebble.'

Then I saw a sharp, thin length of metal, with white gulls attached to it by their feet. I could see that they were in discomfort and pain, and that they wanted to be set free. So that's what I did. I set them free. They flew off. It was a beautiful sight. As they flew, the sharp metal edge became rounded, transforming into a length of driftwood, gnarled and twisted in parts but beautifully smooth. Then the length of wood started to coil up into a circle, and a circular line was formed all the way through the now round piece of wood. That's life – a never-ending circle, not a straight line.

In the distance, I saw a person standing tall. This person also coiled up like the wood, like a baby in its mother's womb. The person was going home. Life is a circular motion, as we are always 'going home'. We are always visiting 'home', as in our spiritual essence.

When we have a realisation, or something suddenly makes sense to us emotionally, spiritually, and physically, that could be something new or something that we might have been considering for years. We suddenly return home to spirit; we touch base. We are closer to understanding ourselves and closer, of course, to God.

Blimey, the words of the song were infusing into my mind! This wasn't just a funeral, this was one of the most singly inspiring, jet propelling experiences of my life! It was a moment when everything made sense all at once! Connections were made in my mind, and my brain was being zapped by answers and realisations! Synapses were fused and unfused, interchanged and sorted, as the neurotransmitters passed from one to the other. I heard the crack as the exchange took place.

When you hear people say, 'I saw my life flash before me,' well, it was sort of like that, but more of an evidential nature. Einstein had his lightbulb moment and Newton saw that apple fall. There it was, done. Most of the answers I had been searching for were there in that one instance! As the song said, 'That atman that I see,' even my feather fizzed!

The problem is that I can't remember exactly what the answers were. My mind has an inability to remember anything important for a period of time that extends an instance! Who would know or even imagine what was happening in all our minds during that time? I, for one, did not know that this would be one of those experiences that would be remembered as one of the most poignant events of my life. Indeed, as a prolific turning point for the immediate procrastinations that would proceed. My future ability to move mountains and to be of use to this world in a way that I, with the biggest, most ridiculous imagination, couldn't possibly begin to know.

My lovely cousin was standing behind me weeping uncontrollably for his father, and I felt hopeless because I couldn't do anything for him. I realised that my hand was still tightly closed on a small, smooth object. I opened my hand and saw the gift. It was a smooth, round pebble with a white line through it.

And from that point on, my two cousins and I each went our separate ways, following similar pathways but with a different pattern! I wonder if they, too, had experienced the moment. I presumed they did.

My uncle's funeral changed my life dramatically for the better. The future now was clear, because questions had been answered. All of a sudden, life's meaning for me was clear, and I knew why I had been born into this world. I understood what I had to do. Imagine that! Well, my sub-conscious knew anyway; I was sure of that!

There was a feeling of great sadness but immense joy. To realise for certain that life is continuous after the physical body has died, to have proof beyond doubt that the spiritual world not only exists, but is as tangible as the material world. In fact, the spiritual world is more real to me and many others than this material world in which we live.

A great change happened inside of me. Seen as written word, this will become as fascinating to some as a science fiction novel. A truth and reality which, up until this point, I existed in and knew about only on a purely subconscious level, in a life in which mostly I struggled, a life where I was happy but not happy, a life in which people knew and loved me but didn't understand me, a life in which I cried and grieved to go home, even when I was at home.

Now I knew I had come home!

12

Ecclesiastic

I felt calm; nothing mattered but the moment.

I was safe, warm, relaxed, sitting in an immense power that I can only describe as peace, perfect peace, and love, perfect love; the love of a universal entire force.

I was myself but not myself; I was myself but not of myself; I was myself but had stepped away from myself, from my body; slightly outside, not fully in. I let this immense power that was safe, that I was protected by, use my vocabulary to operate my voice, to use my physical being, to be able to speak out.

I was asked what my name was.

René I said. He was chuffed. Or was I chuffed? He was proud and happy to be able to speak; the joy showed in his face, the face that was transfigured over mine.

My stomach felt funny. I could feel it, the power, and he was getting power from me.

'What do you do?' I asked.

'I pray', he said.

'Pray?' I queried.

'Philosophy, but in a way that is only obvious to the one who hears. I am like you.

Me?

We are one.

13
The Street

It's been three weeks since my uncle's funeral, and I feel quite numb. Work has been hot and tiring, and I had started to dread the early morning drive. Not only was there the distraction of seeing the other place or time, but recently I had noticed in my peripheral vision some activity of some sort in the drains. There is a rectangular gap on the side of the kerb, which is adjacent to the drain cover itself. I keep seeing movement in this gap. My imagination saw lost or trapped kittens scrabbling to be free of plunging to the murky depths of the sewers below.

Even so, I was glad to get into my car and make the journey home today. I've been meaning to get my aircon topped up, so instead I drove with both windows open and my hair in my eyes.

As I drove into Blossom Road, the smell of barbecue hit my nostrils. I could see that there was a beautiful array of tasty treats and drinks waiting for me! I knew a bit of a do had been planned, but the scene that greeted me made me smile. My neighbours waved to me as I parked, and Trudy told me there was food waiting for me. The young children of the street were running around, and there was excitement in the air. The adults were drinking beer and a special tropical punch, which looked delicious but lethal!

The barbecue was to celebrate the new friendships and bonds that we had all made in the street. The family from Sierra Leone, who were the most recent inhabitants to move in, had laid on some beautiful food. I joined the party and enjoyed the frivolities. It felt so good to forget life for a couple of hours. It was a lovely evening.

I lived in a short, dead-end street. (I mean, there was a large fence at the end, and on the other side were the gardens of the adjacent street.) It seemed like the type of road where, from an outward perspective, nothing much happened. This assumption couldn't be more incorrect. During the twelve years I had been living here, it had been quite the opposite. There had been a lot of 'goings on' in Blossom Road, and even though it looked like a typical terraced street in a city suburb, there was a concentration of strong characters who resided there.

The next morning, the street was unusually quiet; it was a pleasant day in mid-May. My phone said it was 22 degrees, but it felt much hotter in the sun. There was a beautiful cool breeze, and butterflies rose up into my solar plexus. I found myself smiling! I sat in the front room on my computer chair, being mindful of sitting up straight and not slouching. My laptop was on the folded leaf table, with just one leaf up. It's my cosy corner, where I often write in my diary, draw, paint or read, and look up words and meanings in *Roget's Thesaurus* or the *Brewer's Dictionary of Phrase and Fable*.

Today I was going to paint. A cool breeze was floating in from the street, and the front door was held half open by an orange cat doorstop that my mum had made me years ago. Tilly was milling in and out, but mostly lying on the pavement in the shady side of the street, or rolling in the dust and dirt of the gutter. She looked tired and a bit restless.

There was no sound... of traffic, children playing, police sirens, neighbours, or distant conversations. I felt a tingling excitement from who knows where. But I couldn't put my finger on it as yet. Everyone must be having a relaxing day after the festivities of yesterday, when alcohol, food, and laughter had prevailed. I was sure it would get noisier later; it was only 11am!

There are not many times when all the elements are right, but I was in that frame of mind. The conditions were perfect; this was one of those times. I was ready to just see what would happen. I gave the A4 board an undercoat in raw umber, with a dash of white to dilute the strength of the colour, whilst waiting for inspiration. It was instant.

As my brush moved swiftly around the board, I let my hand be guided by the unknown artist, feeling the subtle changes of direction from the free-flowing acrylic paint. I was neither here nor there, when a face appeared from within the dark dimensions. I was entranced as I watched the face build up within the paint. First, a skull appeared, then the flesh formed on top – eyes, nose, mouth, and chin. My hand hesitated as I saw the paint being manipulated in front of me. I held onto the brush but had stopped using it. Then suddenly I was enveloped in colour! Rose pink and tangerine. Lemon yellow, and ochre. I felt so euphoric, and time was no longer. The room filled with a scent of burnt umber, a beautiful organic smell, and I breathed in the colour of the room.

As the paintbrush started to move again and the colourful layers flowed through the brush, I lost myself, not realising that a few hours had passed.

Both peaceful and painful, I painted despair, death, and beauty, turning into torture, suicide, fear, and disease.

Is this the face of The Voice? I thought to myself.

Then The Voice spoke! What it said, well, I just can't remember.

The Voice had surely spoken to me from the face in the picture. I was so certain then, but only minutes later I was not so sure. The tone and words seemed softer, somehow.

I stopped for a nice cup of Earl Grey tea, and fed the cat, who had stopped pacing in and out from the street. People had begun to stir now. Car engines started, doors opened and closed, and conversations flowed on the breeze. This afternoon felt heavenly. There was perfection in the moment.

I drank my tea hot and strong; hunger abated. This was a lonely existence if I couldn't even tell a single person without the worry of being thought insane! If this was real, then I had work to do, and the calling was strong, because a knowledge had been infused in me – a very important message which I had already forgotten. I cried for at least an hour, felt exhausted, then fell asleep.

I awoke from a deep sleep with a ravenous hunger, and slowly dragged myself up from the settee to make some cheese on toast.

14

My New Alarm Clock

What was that? I woke up to a noise and turned to look at my alarm clock. It was a minute before the alarm was set to go off. After a few seconds, I realised the sound was coming from outside the bedroom window, and when I looked, I saw a little bird's feet against the window pane. A pigeon was flying towards the window with its feet angled as if to land, and consequently banging on the window pane with its claws. It did this a few times, and just before it flew away, I noticed that it had a feather in its mouth! One single white, fluffy feather! Wow! How about them apples! What sign was this? Was it just my early morning wake-up call, or a sign with a deeper meaning? I must check and see if there was a nest somewhere. Even if the pigeon was building a nest and had come to the wrong place, it was still a lovely sight to see!

It felt warm. Well, it was the first of June, and about time it started to feel like the summer months were ready to stretch ahead. It was my favourite time of the year, when there is hope in the air. Not just airy-fairy thoughts or dreams that you would wish for, but actual tangible hope! I sensed it around my body, felt a shiver go right through me, and quivered out loud!

I got out of the right side of bed with a spring in my step! The feather felt like it was supporting me, like a rod keeping my back straight, and when I looked in the mirror, I could see a cobalt blue and raspberry haze.

I realised that I had started to feel different lately, and it just dawned on me what that difference was! I actually felt confident for the first time in a long time. I sat in my comfy chair by the bay window, which I had not long painted. It was a fresh crisp area now, with a chair, two cacti, and a mug coaster depicting a guinea pig dressed as the queen. I had a cup of coffee in one hand and my mail in another. I don't receive much through the post, and I tend to throw it into a little basket which sits on top of the meter cupboard, where it's forgotten. But it was time to open it.

I thought back over the last few weeks. Even though I have always acted in a confident manner and given the impression that I am a very capable human being, I have never actually felt that way. I realise now that at this moment I do feel the way that I have been acting for years! How does that saying go? "Fake it till you make it!"'

I looked it up on Google: "…an English aphorism which suggests that by imitating confidence, competence, and an optimistic mind-set, a person can realise those qualities in their real life and achieve the results they seek."

Well, who would know? This new-found feeling was like a weight had been lifted off my shoulders. I had been so used to pretending that I was a certain way, that it never occurred to me how it would feel if life wasn't a struggle. I never imagined what it would be like to genuinely feel this way. It was invigorating, and I hoped it would last.

This alarm phenomena had been occurring on and off for the past few weeks. So I knew that someone was trying to tell me something, but I felt stupid because I didn't know what it was. Nevertheless, I felt elated. The sun had shone for a few weeks, and it only rained in the evenings when the humidity couldn't hold itself in any more.

It was only last week when, as I was fast asleep, my alarm had gone off, and I had switched off both mobile alarms and the alarm clock in my waking daze. I had asked the feather the evening before, just as I was going to bed, to make sure that I woke up the next morning because I had to get my stuff ready for a hospital appointment straight from work.

Blimey, someone made sure I woke up! I heard a loud banging on the outside brick wall of my bedroom, so resounding that it seemed to fill my head, echoing through the house! I looked out of the window, but there was nothing and nobody about.

I also realised the other day that The Voice was quietening down… and had been for a while now! I must have been enjoying the freedom of being without it, and could barely remember that it had been so relevant in my life! That's how it goes, I suppose. It's like being in pain for a long time, and when it stops, the pain is forgotten quickly – like childbirth. Like any pain, really; you think it will never end and it's difficult to see beyond it, and then you're free of it!

Don't get me wrong, The Voice was still around, but I think it must have known it was fighting a losing battle with me! It's been hard, really hard for such a long time, but I don't bore people with the details because it really annoys me when people go on and on about their pain or illness, from a common cold to a serious condition. Unless you are being paid to listen to someone – e.g. a counsellor or a doctor – who wants to know about someone else's pains or problems, and continuous self-indulgent procrastination? You are much more likely to receive help and empathy if you ask for help when you are suffering, and everyone needs attention of that kind at some time in their life.

And so, my life continued as it has done for so long, where a breakthrough was followed by a trial, followed by a release, followed by triumph, followed by contentment, followed by creativity... and so the cycle returned. I learned very slowly, but with flashes of brilliance throughout. *Promise me,* I tell myself, *that this is the time. My time, when creativity comes back as a block of continuous prolific work in its entirety, so I may finally enjoy a prolonged period of harmony, and where I can let my potential be at the forefront of my life, and not trampled by the everyday physicality of this material world which I struggle to be in most of the time.*

I went from feeling anxious and stressed and a reminder of a darker time, to being in the perfect place within half an hour! I was in the perfect place; it was silver, like silver gloopy mercury, and it was silent, and suddenly there was perfect peace. It was hard to come back from, really hard to come back, and I wished I could feel like that all the time. But then, how would I function? I wasn't alone in that place; I was with a healer, and she felt the same. She told me that she always felt this way when she was with me. We complemented each other perfectly and shared this perfect space and time, where time was no longer, where time was infinite, but also did not exist.

15

The Birds

Beauty can appear at the most unusual time, and can be found in the drabbest of places, or at the most cruel and stressful of times.

The last few weeks I had been feeling somewhat lonely. I have known what loneliness feels like in the past, but for some reason this feeling was more of a deep-seated one, a frustration, a fear that there was never going to be anyone who would love me for what I am, never someone to share my life with – a partner, perhaps? It wasn't a physical loneliness in which I was on my own. I had plenty of friends, a son, two brothers, parents, workmates, but this feeling had been creeping up on me for weeks now and had become more prominent in my daily life. I felt disgruntled, discombobulated, uncomfortable, and there was another feeling that I couldn't put my finger on. What was it? It felt like what I would imagine boredom to be like, but I had never been bored before, and I had never felt this exact feeling before, so I wasn't really sure what it was.

It was a warm, wet, dreary day with not much about it, and I was thinking that the flats where I was delivering were becoming dirtier and untidier every day. I climbed the grubby steps one by one to the first floor, noticing the concreteness of it all and the various smells emanating from the flats. I went from door to door, delivering to each tatty letterbox. It was with some distaste that I felt something sticky on my hand, and as I looked to check what it was, at the same time I turned to take the bend to the next delivery point.

I gasped at what I saw! There, perched on the open balcony, was a beautiful sight which lifted my heart! It was a white bird, and it didn't flinch, flutter, or fly away when it saw me, but just stayed watching me. It looked straight at me, as if it was waiting for me to acknowledge it. This bird was slightly bigger than a budgie, rounder and plumper than a robin, with a small orange toucan-like beak, and it was pure white. I had never seen anything like it. I wondered if it had escaped from a pet shop or someone's house. I said, "Hello," and it stayed for a few more seconds, then flew away to my left. I was amazed, and felt pure joy. Now that had really brightened up my day!

For a long time now, I had been noticing the birds more than usual; not my garden birds, which were mostly robins, blue tits, great tits, and sparrows. The occasional magpie some-times dared to come to ground and feed off the larger bits of fat balls, or the tasty blocks filled with insects and mealworms that had been dropped by the greedy squirrel and her sibling. A pair of pigeons visited daily to drink from the tiny bird bath on the rusty wrought iron table. They were too big to fit into the top of the tall, wooden bird table, but it didn't stop them trying. I had a great view from the kitchen sink, and had seen many a risky manoeuvre by the rounded bird trying to land and squeeze itself into the top of the table.

When I was out and about walking the streets, it was the crows, robins, and wagtails that caught my eye. On one occasion, a parrot! But today, it was this unusual bird. Robins often wait for me to enter a garden, and fly so close to my face that they almost brush my nose with their wings. I love the noise of their fluttering. I even had a conversation with a pigeon once. Then, there was a parrot waiting for me on a person's driveway. I saw it before it flew up into the nearest tree. These past few days and weeks, birds such as robins, crows, magpies, and even a squirrel, have come uncommonly close to making contact with my face.

The crows and the ravens, to me, are clever individuals who behave like humans, and they have succeeded in grabbing my attention on many occasions. They don't seem to fly off when I am near them, and I can talk to them. They show me what they are having for lunch, and they fly so close to my face at opportune moments! One crow walked with me as I delivered, and waited at the top of every path of every house in that road for me. It was as if it wanted to help in some way. Or was it trying to tell me something?

The sun had started to try and break through the low clouds as I drove to my next delivery area which was no less untidy. The students' rubbish bags left such a mess that there was always a horde of crows scrapping up and down the messy streets, feasting on the leftover takeaways. This morning, one particular crow was having difficulty opening a container. After noticing him pecking a few slits in the plastic lid and getting nowhere, I sensed his frustration and decided to give him a helping hand. Inside was what looked like the remnants of a Quorn chunk curry. The crows all flocked to the delicious smelling food.

As I carried on down the road, another large crow flew past me in such proximity that it nearly smeared my face with the discarded cheese toastie it was carrying in its mouth! "Look what I've got!" it squawked.

I would love a pet crow, like Cadwaller on Facebook.

16

In the Dark Again

I had enjoyed a light and happy few weeks without The Voice bothering me much. Even when I felt that I was under 'high intensity stress', it never distracted me. Until one day, out of the blue, it started coming back. I didn't acknowledge it for a few days, but it was relentless, gaining momentum and strength, invading my thought process, confusing me, and saying some very upsetting things which manifested into images of a disturbing nature. I had given into it yet again, and yesterday had been particularly gruesome.

As I walked along the road to my first delivery, I crossed at a busy junction. A lorry came speeding past, and an image clouded my vision. I hadn't looked, and the lorry had come too close, knocking me down in one fell swoop. I saw my head roll onto the road. The first thoughts were of my family and friends. Panic took hold of me as I wondered how to get in touch with them before I died. *Would I keep walking and pick my head up? Could I put it back on again, just to make a few phone calls? How would I know where it was?* I really did not need these images running through my mind.

I hoped today would be better. As I walked down the hill to deliver some packages, I hadn't noticed a figure a few metres ahead of me. I was concentrating on whether I had enough time to finish my work before ten past three, as I had to get back to the office. I had agreed to cover a shift because a work colleague had a hospital appointment. At the time, I'd thought it would be fine because it was in the office. I could drink coffee, and eat, and maybe sit down, if it was not too busy. But today had been gruelling, and I just felt I couldn't push my body any more. Everything hurt: my feet, my hands, my back, and my knees. Even though I felt dehydrated, I didn't want to drink much, because there were absolutely no available toilets in this area.

Every step exhausted me more and more, and it seemed like my shift would never end. I stopped briefly to take a sip of water, and realised I had hit a 'brick wall'. Now I could understand what marathon runners meant by that saying! Lately there had been more and more items to deliver and sort every day, and it hadn't let up for weeks. I felt sweaty and dirty and just kept thinking of a cold bath and a chilled beer. I imagined myself drinking an ice-cold bottle of Corona with a lime in the top. I pictured myself sitting in the garden downing the couple of beers that were waiting for me in the fridge at home. I could taste the tang of the lager with the lime infused in the neck of the bottle. Never mind hydrating myself with water. I needed more! I felt like I was drowning in a negative bath of gloop with no way out.

I became transfixed on the figure ahead. The way they walked, their dress style; then, there was no light and there was no hope. I couldn't relax, I couldn't get a thought right in my head: *What was the point of me being alive? Why do I bother trying all the time to become a better person, to do the things that I want to do, because when there is no light and no joy, there is no point?* I felt the pressure in the top of my head, in my forehead, in my sinuses, and behind my eyes. I was worried, stressed, and anxious about the things that needed doing. I had the sensation of tiredness, and the impression of loneliness, and of fear and of neglect. I was experiencing goosebumps throughout my body. I felt like a lost cause. Thoughts buzzed around my head: *I think I need to get a grip, because I am not up to this life. I feel that I am too sensitive for this life. I feel the hopelessness of humanity. I feel the fear of people and animals who are suffering, and I just can't cope with this uncomfortable anxiety.*

I looked at the person ahead and had an unusual thought. *Were these feelings somehow connected with this person?* It seemed so. I couldn't think of anything else. The gap between us had started to widen, so I upped my pace. I needed to know more about this person. I gathered it was a man, but there were no other physical clues. Then it happened. I saw someone cross the street and grab the man round the neck, dragging him into a bush to the left. I think the attacker had a knife or something else in his right hand. My heart was pounding.

'*You are odd! But you also have a special power.*'

'Who said that?' I found myself saying out loud, as I looked around.

I don't think anyone heard me, thank goodness. *I really need to stop doing this, as people will start to talk*, I thought to myself.

With the distraction of The Voice, I had temporarily taken my eyes off the man. When I looked again, he was still ahead of me but much closer. The attacker had disappeared from view, and the man seemed undisturbed by the assault!

I carried on walking behind him, a bit more slowly now, so as not to catch up or overtake him. All the time I was looking out for the mysterious attacker. I had a terrible itch and an irritation on my skin in the area of the feather. It seemed like the feather had gone bad. I imagined the beautiful colours becoming dreary and saw clearly in my mind's eye a brown-grey rotting feather that had started to smell. In fact, I just wanted to sleep and forget it all.

There was a resounding silence inside my head! Then... nothing.

A realisation had just taken hold of all my senses! It hit me physically and stopped me in my tracks! The clarity of it all! Could this be true? That The Voice was not an intrusive thought that could become obsessive and compulsive, but instead, a prediction of sorts? Could The Voice be telling me what was about to happen to this man? Could the reason I was seeing this be, because I, in some future time, will be able to prevent a tragedy, or a violent or abusive action taking place before it happens? By myself? Or with the police? Or some other authority!

Why hadn't I realised this before? It seemed so obvious now! Whenever The Voice speaks, my feather feels heavy and uncomfortable, and my skin feels irritated. This really is a living thing that has to be obeyed!

I had assumed at first that the feather was just a mark, and not a mark of something else – well, not entirely. I knew it meant something more than its physicality, but never knew the entirety, the real depth of meaning to it. Neither did I realise that it was all-consuming! For a time, I thought that the heat which radiated from the feather was an effect from the tattoo being inked into the skin. And even when it lit up, it took a while for it to sink in that this could actually be a living organism within me; separate to me, but of me, at the same time. Did it control me? Or did it just react to me and my thoughts and actions? It really was a curse and a gift at the same time. Whichever way around, the overall result was complete control!

Was I, in some way, intruding on the thoughts and feelings of the person who was walking in front of me? I wondered.

I stopped and pretended to look at my phone. Glancing up, I watched the person walk further and further away from me, and slowly I started to feel the relief as he became a distant speck. I began to feel myself again.

So, was this it? Was this what had been happening all my life? Could it be possible? All I can say is that I have either been totally thick, or it was not meant to be revealed to me, until now. Was this the right time for me to realise? Had I been shown many times, and just forgotten? If it had been communicated to me out of the blue, then my mind would probably not have been able to take this information to be true. I wouldn't have been able to believe that I could do this, without me telling myself that I was imagining it. Or making it all up in my own mind. Because the mind is so strong, and the conscious intellect can tell itself all sorts. It can contradict itself to the point of becoming mentally ill.

Maybe I had to be shown. Or did it have to be sown over a period of time? A whole lifetime? These dark thoughts that I had experienced over many years, was I being taught to manage them and get used to them as being part of my life and in my life? It had taken years for this to be achieved, and only in part. And sporadically...

I don't remember much of the journey driving back to the office, as I couldn't think straight. I looked around me while the traffic lights were at red. It was a beautiful day; I should be glad of that. It was June. The summer months lay ahead. There were things to look forward to. Things could get better, clearer. I was hopeful. Without hope, there is nothing.

Back at the office, I switched off the engine and sat in the car. I was early; well, ten minutes. I wanted to get my head straight before going in and facing people.

For years I had, on the whole, mostly been able to control The Voice, to the extent of it not resulting in the physical manifestation of the dark thoughts. But suddenly, within two weeks, The Voice had started to show more dominant behaviour. Was I feeling out of control yet again? Was this a blip? Was it the inevitable result of being the weaker one in the battle? Would I have to put up with this all my life? Would I experience this constant battle for my mental health, or would the brighter, more positive, productive side, finally win? Or did I now know how to use my unusual way of thinking?

I remembered what The Voice had said earlier: 'You are odd, but have a special power.' Maybe possessing these positive qualities, there was a need to offset them with the darker elements so that I would be able to appreciate all that I had. But I needed to see more positive results lasting for a longer time. These short glimpses of amazing phenomena, for the betterment of mankind, did not satisfy me for long enough. Was this my want over that of others? I do not know.

Did I get perfect inspiration, perfect mindfulness, or pure inspirational thought, only after a splurge of stress or darkness? Only then, did I realise what the suffering was for? So now my mind was used to (or just starting to cope with) these dark thoughts, could I now separate them from myself? Would the clues left to me show me what I needed to be doing to avoid disaster in the future? Was I ready now for when the opportunity arose?

So, first the thoughts, then the premonitions, then the realisation.

I need a holiday.

17
The Fly

There has been a dead fly on the stairs now for three days, and I can't be bothered to pick it up. The house is tidy and relatively clean, but still the fly lies on the stairs. As I step over it, I think of the undone, the unforgiven, and the unfortunate.

I just can't seem to cope any more, I can't handle it, and I panic at the things that seem to be out of my control; things that I think are supposed to be under my control. My computer, for example, doesn't respond to me, especially when I am stressed. I only have to touch it to perform a simple action that I have done a thousand times before, but it seems to not be able to handle the energy that exudes from me. And if I start to get stressed, it just shuts down. In this world of greater technological enumerations, it's hard to be able to do anything at times.

My mind reacts in an obtrusive way and cannot perform the simplest tasks. When one is stressed, this can happen, but I think it's more than that. I can't seem to understand simple concepts in the way others do. I can't seem to be able to function as I should be able to function. When this happens, it just makes me want to evaporate into thin air without a mind, or soul, or conscience, because then I wouldn't have to worry, or feel ill, or feel mentally deficient, or see the pain and feel the suffering of others. I am unable to take it. Even the feather feels brittle at the moment.

I had stuff to do today: pick some things up, make some phone calls, go online. Thank goodness it was my day off; I could take my time. When I finally made it to the front door after much procrastination, it was lunchtime. I took a few deep breaths and opened the door, then winced as the feather contracted. It felt like my skin was being pulled tighter and tighter as I got to the corner of the road.

The day felt motionless. As I walked along the high street, it looked as if the life had been sucked out of everyone – most of all me. Suspended in a grey darkness, Susley looked dreary. I was half expecting one of J.K. Rowling's dementors to come flying towards me! Rain felt imminent, but then again not; it was cool for the time of year, and I felt like crying for no particular reason. Other than having a low-grade virus, I wasn't sure what was wrong with me. I was hopeless with physical illness; it messed with my head. It was hard enough keeping my mind under control when I was well!

It was only three o'clock in the afternoon, but when I looked out from the inside of the card shop for a moment, it looked pitch dark. There was some kind of raucousness outside. An eccentric man – there were many in the area – was shouting loudly. The school kids waiting at the bus stop were laughing, but not goading him. A teenager bounced into the shop with her mate, saying he was scary. I made my way through the gaggle of kids and the impatient adults, and back along the high street to cross at the traffic lights.

These were the lights that I had inadvertently prevented from working one day. That day, I had been stressed to the max. Someone had seriously pissed me off at work, and I had been mulling it over as I pressed the button at the pelican crossing. I hadn't realised how long I and the other pedestrians had been waiting, until I heard someone behind me suggesting that perhaps the lights weren't working properly. I knew by instinct that it was me preventing people from going about their business. It wasn't the first time this sort of thing had happened. So, I decided to move a couple of shops' distance away, and as soon as I did, the lights showed green, and everyone moved on.

Today, though, the lights worked quickly, and as I crossed the road, dodging the on-comers who seemed to be getting out of my way quick fast, I felt better. It was as if being on the other side of the street helped somehow. My phone rang, but I ignored it. I didn't like answering it when I was out, as I needed to put it on speaker phone. There were two reasons for this. Firstly, the phone always made my ear and the side of my face hot, and secondly, I didn't want the germs from my hands transferring from the phone to my face. Putting it on speaker phone was embarrassing, because people listened, and I didn't want to be one of those annoying people that had loud conversations on their mobile in the street.

Suddenly, I spotted someone standing on the corner. They looked towards me as if waiting for me, and beckoned with their hand for me to come closer. When I got to the corner, they had gone, and it was like I was meant to be there. But this had happened three times before now, and I was starting to think I was losing it. *This is the last time I am going to go to the corner*, I told myself, *as I feel like a total idiot and this 'someone' is making me look like one. Today will be the last time I will walk to the corner.*

And it was! As soon as I raised my foot onto the pavement, a dog came shooting out of a side street, and I instinctively caught it, just as a rogue joyrider came blasting round from the next road. I heard a scream, and people around me were muttering and gasping. A woman came running out of her house from the same direction as the dog.

'Thank you so much!' she said. 'You saved Jimmy's life!'

As the woman took her pet from my arms, the only thought that came into my head was that it was a very silly name for a dog.

I realised that I was hungry. Today had not gone as planned. I had got angry that the unexpected had happened. I'd helped, people were upset and happy. I had felt deflated and restless and tried to stop being busy, but I couldn't.

I arrived home, went straight to the record player and put music on, and decided to have at least five minutes sit down. But it was one of those times when I just couldn't let myself be released from the chores that I wanted to do. I made something to eat and hoped that the rain wouldn't come again. I went to bed feeling impatient, then excited, then peaceful and happy. These emotions surged through me at a rapid speed, and I waited in anticipation to experience the next sensation.

18

Conversation With Voice

When I woke up the next morning, I felt ok. Composed. A new week had begun. I realised that other than checking in on my son, I hadn't seen or spoken to any of my friends or family for over a week! I needed to make more of an effort. A cup of coffee, a piece of toast, and I left the house. All was quiet in the street.

When I arrived at work, my manager asked me to take a different route, as someone had phoned in sick. *Change is as good as a rest*, I thought. This morning felt pleasant. As I walked along, I saw a lot of feathers, mostly little white ones, and whichever path I took – whether a pathway of conformity, or as the crow flies – I saw them showing the way. They were always a step ahead of me. I felt comforted and knew that everything would be ok, until The Voice stepped in with a quip or two.

There was a lot of talk about dying today. Dying young, dying too soon, dying horrifically. I always look to the sky for comfort. Today, the clouds were high, mostly cirrus or cirrus stratus. I loved geography in school before it got too difficult.

I always enjoyed when we had lessons about the weather, especially when there was a need for a drawing or two.

I think we are all meant to die old and happy, and not before our time, and not in pain and with suffering. But a lot of the time that doesn't happen. God doesn't want anyone to suffer. Why would God want to take someone before their time? Maybe its denial because I don't want people to die, but I believe this.

'I feel fine, and everything is going to be fine, so shut the fuck up! 'I told The Voice.

The feather pulsated: *'Have you ever thought about talking back kindly to The Voice?'*

'Nope!' I said.

I don't understand life and how it works, even after all these years! I don't know what makes me tick and what makes others tick. Whenever I come to a realisation, a breakthrough, an understanding of life, people, love, and connections, brewing in the background unbeknown to me is another problem more tedious than the last, perhaps more painful, more mentally confusing, more unbelievably upsetting, more logistically difficult for me to comprehend. Perhaps it's because I am on my own. Perhaps that's why we are meant to have someone to live with, to be close to, on hand, and to help when things are tough. But then I'd had that, and it didn't work for me either. No wonder people take their own lives. Same old story, day in, day out, and I never seem to get it right.

'You would think that you'd learn from your mistakes, eventually anyway,' barked The Voice.

'Shut up!' I said out loud, again.

The Voice had been particularly cruel these past few days, gnawing at me with unfailing regularity. I felt an emptiness, a nullity. The feather was throbbing like toothache, so I took some paracetamol. On a more positive note, even though The Voice would disagree, I felt I was getting better at recognising when I have been in a certain predicament before, and even remembering that the last time I hadn't handled it as I would have liked to. And I had been working on myself so that I could advance through life and learn from my mistakes.

But the more problems I solve about this life, the harder the next problem is. I know it's supposed to be like this, but I wasn't sure if I had it in me to handle it. There were times when the answer was 'yes' and times when the answer was undoubtedly 'no'.

19
Sweet Alyssum

It's a beautiful day in July. I was lying on the turquoise settee. There was a fragrant scent of sweet pea and alyssum flowing through to my nostrils, drifting in from the garden via the open door. Ahhh… summer, I love it! It was 26 degrees with a cool breeze, hot in the sun, but cosy in the shade. Whenever I got back to the house, I always felt glad. I love being at home as much as I love the outdoors.

My house wasn't steeped in the longitude of a lifetime of living in it, like my parents' house was. Even still, it has a wonderful atmosphere about it, and most people who come in say they like the feel of the house. Even though I have lived here almost 12 years now, it still seems a temporary abode, though I have no intention or inclination to move. It's as if I know somehow that I won't be spending the rest of my life here. Yet I still feel settled. I like the homely, peaceful feeling, the easiness of keeping a small city back garden, the variety of neighbours, and the host of animals inside and out.

There have been new sounds in the garden these past couple of weeks – a high-pitched whistle and different accents. I think someone must be training a puppy in their garden, or teaching a cat to return home on the sound of the whistle. I couldn't quite make out the name of the animal being called. There were new neighbours next door-but-two on one side, and next door-but-three on the other. New voices, music, and sounds for the summer, as well as the usual cockerel, duck, and various other birds who grace me with their songs.

The magpie has been eating all the mealworms that I put out for the smaller birds, and the pigeon clears up all the seeds from the gravel, which have spilt while the birds take a sunflower seed or two. The squirrel always takes the fat ball I put out, but no-one eats the peanuts. It was such a pity that soon I would have to get up from my relaxing repose and get my stuff ready for the meeting.

I have never really hung around before – well, not as an adult, anyway. There has been no room in my head or my life for hanging around. The meeting was usually a six-thirty start, but it had been changed this time, and no-one seemed to know if it started at seven or half past.

I waited on the corner, in my car with the air con on (finally got round to getting it topped up!), to collect a packet of gluten-free digestive biscuits and a tenner. It felt dodgy, because I was in the exact spot where a car appeared most evenings to sell a ten-pound draw to one of my neighbours.

Beep, beep! It was the notifying but not too intrusive beep coming from the car on the corner – usually a small black car, conspicuous by its black windows. The skunk mobile was here! There was a time when it honked its horn at 11pm or later, and once I shouted obscenities out the window at them, in no uncertain terms telling them where to go! The two young men were rather surprised! I don't know why; perhaps it was my aggressive vulgarity!

I wasn't looking forward to this evening. There was a lot to discuss, and I hadn't gathered the information that I said I would at last month's meeting. I was helping Lisa with her School PTA meetings by taking minutes and other bits 'n' bobs, because the actual secretary was on maternity leave. Lisa got me embroiled in projects every now and then. I wasn't particularly interested in some of them, but I really enjoyed being in her company.

I was thinking up my excuses, when along came my son's father with the biscuits and the tenner, which he was lending me. He had probably procured it by some illicit deal, and I would use it to pay the window cleaner, who would in turn pay the dealer at the corner of the road, whose spot I was in.

The meeting went well. Lisa made me laugh, we ate the biscuits, drank tea, and put the world to rights via the Parent Teacher Association. Luckily, I didn't have to make any of the decisions or vote on anything, because I was just taking the minutes. Also, they seemed to forget that I had promised to research the costs and places for first aid courses for groups. I could handle that.

The other members of the committee seemed pleasant enough and made me feel welcome, although I never feel fully part of any group or team. When you feel very different, there's always something missing that prevents a real closeness, or a real bond from forming. It's getting slightly better, because at certain times I can feel involved. But it takes years of practice to be able to drop anything and go straight into a different source or zone. To be in a different frame of mind, or on a different level of thought, so to speak.

20

The Void

It was hot! And I mean hot. Twenty-nine degrees had been predicted today. It was half eight in the morning, and already warm and beautifully sunny. As the time went by, a warm but refreshing breeze was available in the shade.

My sunny disposition wasn't out, though. I felt the same, almost, as I had for over a week now – 11 days, in fact. I had more energy today because all I'd done all week was sleep whenever I could. Go to work, then sleep, wake up, do tea, sit in the garden, then sleep. I realised that I still hadn't been in contact with my friends, but then, after a pang of guilt, I thought, *Well, they haven't contacted me!* Meet friends, then sleep, wash my hair, and fall asleep whilst deciding to dry it. I didn't know exactly what was wrong, but I felt so sad, and I felt nothing at the same time. The void was back.

It has come more often lately, and this time it seems to be lasting longer. I feel as if nothing is worthwhile and that there is no point to anything at all. I have friends, family, interests, work, and voluntary work, but there suddenly doesn't seem any point to my existence whatsoever.

I woke up on a Wednesday morning feeling like this! Just as suddenly as it appears, the void can disappear, but this one did seem different. My emotions are too complex to decipher, and today it felt like maybe there was some light at the end of the tunnel.

The struggle I feel when the void takes me over is so hard to put into words. It's like a depression, but knowing that there is actually no need for me to feel this way. There is no justification for struggling to do the things I need to do. No rationale for all the effort it takes me to decide to do the things that I always do, and mostly enjoy. There was an irritation that came with this feeling – a feeling that I wanted and needed to be alone, yet felt incredibly lonely at the same time. I craved to be with friends.

I would like someone around who I could rely on, and not have to be the one that others rely on. It would be nice to have a companion who was actually bothered about me. But at least summer was here, because it helps when the sun is out, and I can at least potter in the garden, or go for a bike ride, or spend time outdoors.

For a period of time after I do the work I was meant to do, I always feel great! I am happy, contented, satisfied, and uplifted. To know that I have helped others in a practical, mental, and emotional way, what better feeling can one have? I will never cease to be amazed! When I put my talent and gift to work in unison with the beautiful ones who protect me, and who help me and others, it works! What else could be better? Nothing, because this is why I was made!

But who made me? Who put this feather on my back? I always asked a lot of innocent questions when I was a child, and quite a few fiery questions when I was a teenager. There was one occasion that I will never forget. It was one of the many times I asked about the mark. My mum was fuming and didn't speak to me for weeks! Not properly, anyway. She walked out of the house and didn't come back for ages. I thought that was it.

'How dare you go ahead with something like that without talking to me first!' she had screamed.

I don't remember my exact reply. There was a lot of confusion on that day. She couldn't bear to look at me. My dad just rolled his eyes and tried to take the sting out of my mother's cruel words and actions. To this day, I don't know how she could think that I had been and had this tattoo done by myself! I was only 11!

My burning curiosity remained, but as the answers were not forthcoming, the questions became less and less frequent, until I finally gave up and just got on with life.

This morning, I had slept through three alarms again! The only thing that awoke me in just enough time to get to work was a voice calling my name. I thanked whoever it was, and rushed about trying to get to work without looking completely just-woken-up kind of obvious! I tried to rub the cheek creases off my face, but to no avail. I can usually get myself dressed, washed, and teeth cleaned in 15 minutes flat, but that is when I am fully awake, after sitting in bed slowly opening my eyes to a cup of coffee.

Today, it wasn't that busy at work, thank goodness, so maybe I would be able to get home early and snuggle up in bed reading a book. I don't think there's any point in even thinking of doing more than the bare minimum to survive today. That's how bad I feel.

I struggled to walk in a straight line as I made my way along. I looked over to the other side of the busy main road to see if Rose, a long-time elderly friend of mine, had her windows open. She lived above the Co-op, in a flat that was expansive, more like a house really. The windows were open, but I couldn't get her to answer the phone; sometimes she fell asleep or didn't hear it. I suddenly felt the need to see that she was ok, just to wave at her.

The steps were steep on Church Road. Most of the houses had around seven stairs down to the front door. I don't know which is worse, steep steps up, or steep steps down. My balance was a little off today, and I lost it at the top step and started to fall. I panicked. Disastrous consequences flashed through my mind as my legs struggled to find footing, now a few steps down. The panic left and, in its place, I could see everything. Omnipresence of the mind. Just like the character in the film Limitless, I was blind but now I see. Those times when your mind is so clear; I knew what I needed to do and just how to do it. At the same time, I felt someone else take my place! Someone with longer legs than me! They reached the steps and landed for me! Until I caught up with them.

'Fucking hell, that was close,' I spat, as I landed on firm ground.

My heart was pounding and my breathing shallow, as someone came to the door. Their dog had been barking. They looked embarrassed and confused when they opened the door. I tried to maintain some sort of composure, but my physical state needed some sort of explanation. I told the woman that I had tripped coming down the stairs, but wasn't hurt. My feather was red, my face was red, and I wanted the ground to swallow me up. I left the premises somewhat shocked. My eyes felt like they were popping out of my skull.

'Thank you so much,' I whispered.

21
The Summer of Cats

When I arrived home, I made a cup of tea and rang Rose again. Her son answered. He told me that Rose had had a fall earlier today, down the steps from the flat. Luckily, her fall had been broken by a mattress at the bottom of the fire exit stairs. Someone had fly-tipped overnight.

It was a long way down those steps! When the paramedics arrived, they said that there were no obvious broken bones, but that she needed an x-ray to make sure. Rosie had refused to go to hospital, so was at home in bed. I said that I would pop in and see her later.

This was the 'Summer of Cats'. There was Cat no. 1, Cat no. 2, Cat no. 3, Cat no. 4, and Cat no. 5.

Cat no. 1 lived a few doors down towards the high street, and was a young cat who was out most days playing in the street, chasing moths and feathers, and sitting on top of cars basking in the sun. Her name was Tilly.

Cat no. 2 appeared that summer when a young family moved in across the road. He was a very handsome Siamese cat who, on first appearance, seemed very aloof and would bite or swipe if offended. But once you got to know him, he was a very warm, loving cat, with watery blue eyes and a rather large, long, but elegant nose. He loved attention. As soon as he moved into our road, he made pretty sure that the other cats on the block knew who was boss! He made a funny noise, as if he was continually clearing his throat, and he was rather old and scrawny. His name was Billie Bob.

Cat no. 3 was big and fluffy, black with white socks and a perfect white moustache. She looked quite wide-eyed and jumpy, but seemed to want to come inside and explore the area – especially liking my bed for naps during the day. I called her 'Fluff Ball Fucker'. She was quite annoying. She was a cat that if it were a woman would be wearing dolly-red lipstick; you know, the cheap kind that smudges because of over-application. She would have droopy eyes and an expression of distant hope.

We had competition from the boy in the orange top for the attention of cat no. 3. He came from nowhere really. I started noticing him on the corner of the street occasionally, until it came to the point that he was there every single day. He must have been about 12, and he wore a bright orange top. It was around the same time every day, when the kids in the road returned from school. He loved Cat no. 3 and would smooch her and talk to her. Some of the neighbours thought he might be visiting the boys at no 30. But we found that this was not the case. He disappeared as quickly as he appeared, and we never knew where he came from or went.

Cat no. 4 came near the end of the summer, and was rather large, with very long legs and lots of energy. I called him 'Choochie Face'.

A couple of years ago, Cat no. 1 moved into my house. I think she was sick of being unable to get into her house when she wanted to. Especially when it was raining or cold, or she needed to get away from the other cats. A new cat, no. 5, who I called 'Pirate' had started to bully her. After being a frequent visitor for all that time, she decided that she wanted to make her stay permanent.

After a lot of deliberation on my part, and constant visits to her family home to return her late in the evening – so that I could go to bed and so that her owner didn't worry – I finally gave up. It was after a few evenings in a row in the week of the fifth of November, when she had spent all week terrified by the noise of the fireworks and hiding under my chair. One night, in an instant, after saying for a few years that she was not my cat and that she had to go home, I decided that she could move in if that's what she wanted. Her owner didn't even notice that Tilly was now sleeping at my house. After a couple of months, her owner said, 'Oh well, she goes where she wants,' and promptly moved house without Tilly.

I have always been grateful that she has chosen this home to lay her head and for her company, but I don't know whether one day she might decide to move on.

The new cat that I called Pirate has been visiting frequently and is a bit of a nuisance to Tilly. He has a harsh, unfriendly face, and is black and white with a funny black fringe, like a haircut from a pastry bowl. He has a little black goatee beard. He is a he, I think, and quite hefty in size, with a weird loud meeoooowww that is drawn out and sounds angry. He has decided by the looks of it that this house is available for naps and shelter from the rain at any time of the day or night – to the detriment of Tilly, who is ousted out of her own home to meow in the rain!

I returned from work one day to find Pirate curled up on my new cool blue stool, while poor Tilly was standing out in the rain waiting for me! The neighbours have told me that frequently Pirate has been seen sitting chilling in my window – after chasing Tilly out in to the street, I presume. Sometimes Tilly is in luck, because she is asleep upstairs, unbeknown to Pirate, while he is downstairs. I am not happy about this situation, but Pirate always makes a bolt for the cat flap as soon as I turn the key in the door.

During this 'Summer of Cats', the police may as well have set up a little shed at the bottom of the road and taken it in turns to wait until something happened and then pop out. It would certainly have saved on resources, petrol, and energy for them. Usually, the police don't seem to be around anywhere, and even if you call them, they don't actually appear in person. I am sure they are now a figment of everyone's imagination.

One time, before Dawn lived at number 28, a couple moved in there. I was in the street talking to Trudy and playing ball with the kids, when I saw the man and woman leaving their house. As soon as I set eyes on the couple, I felt angry. I didn't want them in the street.

In my head, I heard the word 'Murderer'.

A feeling just suddenly came over me, and I felt that one of them had murdered someone! It just came out of the blue! My feather stung and I didn't understand why at the time.

I told myself to ignore the feeling, but months later, Trudy told me some gossip that I wished I had never heard. The woman at number 28 had told her that someone had died by her hands and that she hadn't meant it to happen. A week later, they were moved out.

Another time, the local supermarket round the corner on Silver Birch Road had been held up at gunpoint. The two thieves had run around into our little street, with a policeman hot in pursuit. They hadn't realised that it was a dead end, so they had to jump over the six-foot fence at the bottom of the road. How they did it, I don't know, but their urgency was greater than the solitary policemen, as he didn't quite make the jump.

On another occasion, I arrived home one summer's day, and Trudy from no. 1 approached me with a grin. Apparently, Dawn was chasing one of her elderly clients down one of the side streets, shouting obscenities and whipping him with his own belt. Trudy had asked her if she was ok, and the reply was that she couldn't speak now because she was working. We laughed so hard and wondered how long the chase had been.

22
Hot Days

It was twenty-nine degrees!

There was a hot breeze as I walked to the bus top, but there was no air on the bus even though I sat by the window. I breathed slowly in but could only feel stillness and heat. It would have been cooler to walk the couple of miles, maybe catch a bit of shade under the trees or a slight breeze, but I was running late. I had been working all day, so I'd taken a change of clothes to work so I could go straight out to save time.

I can't complain, though. It was a long, hot summer. I had got my wish! It was reminiscent of the summer holidays from school. Life seemed good then, the school holidays stretched out before me, and I played in the street until 11pm. I am sure in those days the light of day lasted much longer.

It had been hot now for about a month, and three weeks since we'd seen any rain. City heat is so different from seaside heat. I am glad of the trees. Neasing was a big city, but the surrounding suburbs were filled with trees and parks, canals and rivers.

Perhaps a cocktail would cool me down and pep me up. I was meeting a few mates for a bite to eat and a couple of drinks for Janet's birthday. There would be the usual suspects, plus a few newbies from Jenna's new place of work. These are the girls I have known since our kids were little. We used to meet up after playgroup in the local café, and have been friends ever since. I call them the 'Café Girls'. It was definitely time to catch up with everyone. I wore my new sandals, had painted my toenails, put on a summery top, and some long, baggy shorts.

My moisturiser was oozing out of my face in the heat, and my lipstick felt like it was slowly slipping off my lips. I was glad to get off the bus.

When I arrived, I saw Janet sitting at one of the tables outside The Lounge. It was in the busy little centre of Susley, somewhat reminiscent of Notting Hill as it was pictured in the film, where Hugh Grant met Julia Roberts. It even had a private park. I waved back and went to sit with her. She always liked to secure a few tables when there was going to be a group of us meeting up.

'Grab those two chairs,' she ordered. 'Megan and Jenna will be arriving shortly.'

'Who's coming altogether?' I asked, pulling the chairs over to the table.

Janet took another drag of her cigarette before replying. She always seemed to be able to smoke like it took her no effort at all, and as if she wasn't really inhaling anything.

'Well, Megan, Becky,' another puff, 'then Jenna may come straight from work.' Exhale. 'Also Nat. '

I sat down.

'I think a couple of Jenna's' workmates may be meeting her here and bringing a new puppy,' she went on. 'Nat's here, but she's popped over to Sainsbury's to get some nappies for Maisie.' Nat, Janet's daughter, had been only 16 when she became pregnant with Maisie, but she was a great mum.

Janet was my closest friend out of the Café Girls. As soon as we met, we got on as if we had known each other for years.

'Oh, ok,' I said. 'I'm just going in to get a drink. What you having?'

'I'm fine for the moment,' Janet said, pointing to her large glass of rosé with just a dash of soda and ice.

'Ok, will get you a birthday cocktail later.'

I decided that a raspberry and prosecco cocktail was in order. I felt light and happy, but I needed to get up for work in the morning so didn't want to get too tipsy. I feel too old for hangovers, and I definitely didn't want to get up feeling rough for work! My mates had a tendency to stay up late drinking and not caring about getting up in the morning, especially on a Friday when they had a lie-in, but I didn't! I always felt their disappointment when it was time for me to go and they were staying. Sometimes I missed the best part of the evening; though, sometimes the worst!

As we sat chatting and waited for the others, I gave Janet her pressie. It was only little. We never bought each other expensive gifts. Janet loved costume jewellery and she couldn't get enough of it. Her bedroom was full of it, along with clothes and shoes, some which she had never worn. When she was in full time employment, she would hit the shops after work every Friday. Then go on to the pub.

The evening was really enjoyable, and as more people arrived, we were persuaded by Jenna to go inside. She was hungry and wanted to get a table before they got taken. Jenna was usually pissed before she arrived anywhere, but today, coming straight from work, she was refreshingly sober.

'I need a drink,' she said, approaching the bar.

'What you having?' I asked. She could never decide on wine or beer. It was usually wine, but she became very drunk very quickly on wine and made very bad choices.

'You choose,' she said.

I suggested a cocktail, knowing that she couldn't afford to keep drinking them. That way, the decision to choose wine or beer wouldn't be mine.

During the meal, I became increasingly aware of a young man sitting on a bar stool by a pillar...

'I'm talking to you, Anna!' said Janet.

'Sorry, I was miles away,' I replied. 'I think we should go!'

'What? Who you looking at?' she asked.

'That young man behind you, but to your left. Don't look straight away,' I ordered. 'He's with a group of people.'

'What about him?' replied Janet.

'Well, I saw a knife stuck in the pillar behind him, just above his head,' I whispered.

'A knife?' she said, looking confused. She turned round in an obvious way, and I swore.

'Janet!'

'Ok, ok, he didn't see me,' she said, rolling her eyes and giggling. 'I can't see a knife.'

'It's not there now, but it was,' I told her.

'How many of them have you had?' she said, and laughed as she glanced at my second cocktail.

Janet was used to my unusual quirks and took me just the way I was. She always said that I never judged people the way others did. I was grateful for that.

We brushed the conversation aside and carried on enjoying the evening. There was lots of laughter, and I thoroughly enjoyed myself. Eventually, it came to that time, and I hated that I would soon have to leave.

When I felt I had better make a move, inevitably I was scorned for leaving early because I had to get up for work. I said my goodbyes, which were met with some resistance because of the earliness of my parting, but I insisted I had to go.

'So have I,' said Megan, with a hint of disdain. 'Stay for one more drink. We'll be going soon ourselves.'

But I headed off, knowing too well that they had no intention of getting home anytime soon, work or no work. Luckily, I had the excuse of walking Janet's daughter and the baby partway home, because the little one was getting restless. Walking had to be at Nat's pace, which was at speed, because she wanted to get the baby home before she needed her bottle.

The baby giggled all the way, past the park, past the police station, and then the shops. I walked home the long way round so that I could be in her company a while longer, then we finally parted on the corner. She didn't have much further to go, and I offered to walk her all the way back, but she said she would be fine.

When I got home, I had a bar of chocolate and a cup of Earl Grey tea in bed. A perfect end to a lovely evening.

As I drank my tea, knowing I would regret eating all this chocolate, I started to doze off then heard the distant sound of buzzing. It was getting nearer and nearer, louder and louder, and I became uncomfortable with the sound of its proximity. What was that? It had become more of a thudding noise. I realised that it must be a police helicopter searching, because the sky outside had become brighter.

A slightly panicked thought crossed my mind: *Is it going to crash into the house?*

I was about to get out of bed to look out the window, when a brilliant light dazzled me. The police helicopter had lit me up as I was sitting in bed! I put my forearm up to shield my eyes, but it seemed to stay there forever. *Well, this is embarrassing, they must be having a bloody good laugh at my expense!* I told myself. It felt like there was a giant peeping Tom looking in at me. Eventually, it started to pull away, and the noise and light slowly became a distant memory.

'Dear God, that was intrusive!' I shouted in defiance.

23
Mr Rahmanzai

Oh no! For goodness' sake! This is all I need! I was running late, and The Godfather was on his doorstep, pointing and talking to one of the neighbours. I had seemed to faff around more than usual this morning, then as soon as I got to the front door, this happened!

Just go for it, I told myself, *say you're in a rush and you can't stop. Don't give him the opportunity to get a word in.* I took a deep breath and must have left the house more boldly than I realised, because I made The Godfather and his associate jump when I opened the front door with gusto.

'Hi, can't stop, running late!' I blurted out.

The Godfather looked surprised as I spoke, but carried on chatting.

'Well, you have embarrassed yourself completely,' said The Voice.

I agreed.

As I walked briskly to the end of the road and turned the corner, there was Mr Rahmanzai!

'Hello!' I said, much too enthusiastically. 'You ok?'

Now, I wouldn't have minded stopping for a quick chat with Mr Rahmanzai.

'Greetings,' he replied, with a bow of the head and a dignified smile.

I felt my feather leap on my back as we passed on the street. We didn't often bump into one another, but when we did, it felt good. Along with a few others, I had rented a property from Mr Rahmanzai several years before. At the time, I had just left college, and a few of us needed a place to live. In those days I didn't mind sharing a kitchen, living room, and bathroom. Mr Rahmanzai lived next door, and I remember having a few good philosophical discussions with him. I also got on really well with his daughters. Most of us paid our rent on time and kept the place tidy.

He was very laid back for a landlord. There was one incident when a party got out of control, and one of the lads drank too much and started ripping the fence down for more wood for the bonfire. Mr Rahmanzai appeared at the party, and I remember offering him a can of lager, amongst the chaos. He was trying to go upstairs at the time, because there was a report of someone peeing in the bath. I don't think he knew about the fence at that point. He remained his usual dignified self and declined on the beer, saying that he didn't drink. He never raised his voice or called the police. He had more important things on his mind.

Then one day, not long after the party, I saw him out of context.

Mr Rahmanzai was burning books in the town square. He spotted me through the hubbub of the crowd, so I waved at him. He looked surprised but nodded in response. I had a bit of a crush on Mr Rahmanzai. I carried on walking, thinking that my rent was due, and smiling to myself as I recalled an incident in the supermarket a few weeks previously. I had been perusing the different types of cheese; I couldn't go a day without a bit of cheese, and fancied something different. I decided on Red Leicester, and as I turned to go to the bread counter, a group of women in full burka and hijab surrounded me. There were four in total, and I was aware of onlookers as I was enveloped. There was giggling, and one said, 'Guess who?' I laughed and said, 'Mr Rahmanzai daughters?' The giggling continued and we embraced. I noticed a look of amusement from one of the onlookers.

Now, after passing Mr Rahmanzai, I carried on walking down Silver Birch Road, deep in thoughts and memories. My shift had been cancelled today. The manager had called to say that I wasn't needed, as they had enough staff. The person I was supposed to be covering for had been able to come in after all. He asked if I minded, and said he could always make up my hours next week. Usually this would annoy me, especially as I could have stayed out longer last night. But today I was glad of the free time.

I think I was smiling when I heard, 'Someone's happy today.'

I looked across the street and saw Janet. She had a shopping bag in each hand.

'I was just thinking about you!' she said. 'You'll never guess!'

'What's that?' I asked as I crossed over to her side of the road.

'Last night!'

'It was good, wasn't it?' I replied.

'Yes,' she said, 'but I mean something happened.'

'What, after I left?' I thought of Jenna getting drunk and making a fool of herself, or getting into trouble somehow.

'No, well, yes. I mean, this morning on the news.'

'What?' I was getting confused.

'A young man was stabbed on his way home, somewhere between the centre of Susley and the high street. The report said that his friends had only just left him, and they had all been in The Lounge! Didn't you hear the police helicopter?'

My feather leapt and suddenly I felt like crying. I had completely forgotten last night's events – the young man, the knife above his head, then the helicopter. The world suddenly seemed smaller. My solar plexus dropped down somewhere towards my feet. I needed to take a deep breath.

'Is he ok?' I asked.

'He's in hospital, they said,' Janet replied. 'The police are appealing for witnesses.' She looked at me more closely. 'Why aren't you in work?'

'Cancelled,' I replied with a shrug.

Janet was an avid listener of the news, both local and worldwide. Nothing seemed to pass her by. I was the opposite. I didn't like knowing, unless it was positive. Janet had a penchant for depressing or tragic events. I don't know why, because they stressed her out and depressed her. But I was glad she had told me this.

'That knife you saw! I have shivers down my spine!' she said as she lit a cigarette in the street. She looked pale. 'You're bloody weird, you are!' she added.

We laughed. But I felt as if I listened to us from a distance, and they were both very nervous laughs.

24
The Cat Walk

The paint was watery. The tin had been left outside and had rusted. I stirred it with a plant cane, but it seemed to take forever for the paint to arrive at a suitable consistency. This was my second attempt at painting the old wooden bench, which was flaking and rickety. Last time, it had started raining, or I just ran out of time; I can't quite remember. But then, remembering seemed to be tricky for me at the moment.

The bottom of the can was leaking. So, I put it into a bucket and attempted to clean the cobalt blue paint that had seeped onto the paving slab, using a garden brush and a watering can full of rainwater to wash it all into the drain.

It was an idyllic morning – a beautiful Sunday in August – and I glanced at the weather app on my phone. At that moment it was 18 degrees. There was a cool breeze and some cloud. A distant ice cream van seemed to have been doing the rounds forever, with its Yankee Doodle chimes. And someone was playing light jazz, the kind you get at an afternoon fête. I felt satisfied that I had had some company with friends the other night, but was worried about the young man and the knife. I felt very alone. Even the cat was fast asleep upstairs on my bed.

The sound of the brush strokes soothed my mind as the blue paint dripped doggedly onto the bin bags which I had scattered haphazardly on the floor.

I heard an irritated voice in the distance, from one of the neighbours. A young mum was telling her toddler off.

'Stop following me round!' she yelled.

When the toddler moaned a reply, the mum shouted, 'Or go inside then!'

It was getting hotter; insufferable, some would say. But I would cope with any heat to say that we were having a decent summer. It had been 33 degrees in some parts of the UK of late, but today it was definitely cooler. Suddenly bored with the painting, I pottered round the garden, then went up the alley at the side of the house, carrying my leaking tin of paint round to the back.

Blimey! Down the alley was almost impassable for the weeds and the ivy growing from next door. It was supposed to be a fire exit for six houses. I decided to clear a path of sorts and pull up the weeds. It was a relatively easy job, as the weeds came out with little effort, and even the roots emerged with some of them. As I got down to the adjacent horizontal part which connected some of the houses, it was a different story, though. A pile of weeds that I had extracted a couple of months earlier were now nicely dehydrated in a pile, but a mass of ivy and sticky and spiky nettles had now overtaken the area. I started to sneeze as I cut down the ivy and the stingers. Tiny, sticky pods were attaching themselves to my t-shirt, but I managed to cut through a sort of archway in the ivy, so at least if there was a fire, the route was passable.

I moved on in the list of my garden chores to painting the outside of the fence. The inside of the fence had been lovingly painted two years ago by me and two helpers. Then last year, the second coat had been applied. Today, the part which faced the alley was in need of its first coat, so here I was. I realised I had left the leaking blue tin of paint in the bucket at the back of the alley. *I'll get it later*, I thought to myself.

As I grabbed the plastic tub of fence dye, the doors of the little garden cupboard (which I had found in a skip. Bargain!) fell open. It had a broken door catch, but the fence paint was being used as a door stop. A baby rat flew out and scuttled off through the garden and under the fence, closely followed by Tilly. She then scrambled quickly up to the top of the fence, losing her balance, and dropping down the other side to the back alley.

'Shit! Tilly!' I shouted.

I was worried that she had landed in the bucket of paint I had left there, so I ran round to see. Tilly looked ok, but her pupils were huge. Thankfully, the rat had escaped her clutches. But when she turned around, I saw that the tip of her tail was blue! A beautiful cobalt blue. It looked good, actually!

'Ah, you silly thing,' I told her. 'Come on, we'll go inside and wash your tail.'

It was a struggle, as Tilly was not the most docile of cats. I put the tip of her tail under the tap, as she scrambled onto the top of my head, scratching the side of my face.

'Ok, ok,' I soothed. 'There's nothing to be scared about, calm down.'

I managed to grab a piece of kitchen roll and wipe her tail before she ran out into the garden. I didn't want her to wash it off herself in case it poisoned her. *I got most of it off, though*, I thought to myself as she scuttled off.

Back at the fence, I carried on with the job in hand. The dye splattered to the ground with a blunted drip-drop kind of noise. It was so quiet in the alley. No cries of children in the near distance, not much noise from the adjacent main road, no chattering of adults over fences, and no music playing. As I painted, watching the now sea green colour sink into the wood of the fencing panel, I became lost in thought. As the watery dye covered the panels, I noticed that the light covering of moss which had formed on parts of the fence, at first held a waterproof resistance. I persevered until the moss yielded its invulnerable defiance.

I couldn't be bothered to scrub the moss off separately. At one time I would have done, but now I am a different person. I don't believe in wasting time, especially if it disturbs my rhythm. Sometimes a job can be done just as well, even though a step or two of the process has been missed out. Nowadays, I am very fond of the saying: 'Needs must while the devil drives.'

This is maybe more profound than at first thought. Perfection versus imperfection.

There's a lot to be said about not wanting or expecting perfection, and just doing what you can at the time. I must have wasted so many minutes, hours, days, years even, wanting perfection in everything I did. If that couldn't be achieved for whatever reason, then I just abandoned it, or just never started. It took me years to realise that I could get a lot more done and achieved by not expecting things to be perfect. Even now I can easily slip back into the idea of can or can't, and not giving myself a choice of anything in between.

I recently read an article about left-handed versus right-handed people, and how the different sides of the brain are used. I wondered, *Would I think differently as I changed hands from left to right with the paintbrush?* As I was pondering this, I started to feel uncomfortable, as if I was being watched.

I turned my head to the left, and there was Pirate sitting at the top end of the alley, in mid-position, watching me. This was a cat who didn't seem to blink and had a way of making me feel uncomfortable. Sometimes I would get up in the middle of the night and he would be sitting at the top of the stairs, looking at me as if he had been there all night in the same spot of my field of vision, waiting for me to enter it. It was odd and downright creepy.

Just then, Tilly came to the back gate, and a staring match of locked eyes and low cat calling began. The sky had clouded over with cumulous nimbus, and I wanted to get the paint to dry before the cats started to use their walkway on the top of the fence and get their paws wet.

25
Festival Day

I still felt lonely, and today even more so. These isolated moments are mostly in the summer, or when the weather is particularly lovely for the time of year. A crisp day in autumn, or a blue sky, frosty day in winter, can have the same effect on me. I always feel that it is such a waste of one's life to be inside when the sun is shining. I just can't bear to be indoors if I haven't spent at least a few hours out of doors each day.

It was now afternoon and comfortably warm in the shade of the alleyway. The morning's clouds had drifted away, and the sky was blue. I was pleased because the paint on the fence would dry quickly. My phone said it was only 23 degrees, but it felt so much hotter in the sun. I was glad I had put a vest top and a hat on to paint the fence.

There was a local festival in the afternoon, which was an annual event. In comparison to the morning's peace, I could already hear the voices of excited children, parents shouting out to be careful, and the throbbing bassline of the music. A few sirens could be heard in the distance, and alarms were going off. Then there was the revving of car engines, motorbikes, and the beeping of horns. It was these noises that were making me feel lonely. They were sounds of joy and fun, just people enjoying each other's company. I thought of past years, and realised that there had only been one single time when I had actually spent a few hours at the festival with my mates.

Being outside when there is a particular destination, or a chore to do, or just for enjoyment, is a natural process for me, but it's a different feeling when I want to go outside because of an event, when to go alone would feel too lonely. Whereas a walk in the park and a cup of coffee with a book, or my phone, is an enjoyable feeling, for some reason to walk around a festival on my own is not. Festivals are best enjoyed in a group of two or more, and definitely not alone.

In previous years when I would ask friends to come along, it never went well. One year, I met up with Jenna, who was already there with a group of people I didn't really know. Usually, that doesn't faze me at all, but that time it did. So, I made my excuses after an acceptable amount of time that didn't seem rude, and left. Last year, I was supposed to meet up with one of the neighbours, Trudy. She said she would let me know when she was leaving her house, but she didn't even text. And when I invited Janet, she couldn't make it because she was going to stay with her fella for the weekend.

Whatever the reasons, the results are the same. Another year spent either not going to the festival, or going alone, because no-one could be bothered to come with me. I always felt like I didn't have any friends on festival day, that when it came down to the crunch there was not one person who cared enough to spend any time with me and an acute loneliness enveloped me. The reasons no-one ever wanted to go with me were varied. There were many excuses. Yes, it was busy, and there were too many people in close proximity to each other. You could never get served at the pub it was centred around, but it was worth popping by for an hour at least. My friends either didn't enjoy the crowds, or were busy, or were too lazy to walk there, as there were definitely no car parking spaces in the Susley area around or near to the festival.

I usually didn't let the loneliness beat me, and would take a walk through the festival area by myself, stop to have a quick chat, or say hello to people I met as I wandered through. People were usually in little groups of their own, or couples spending a nice day together. There was always live music, food that I couldn't eat, and a few independent stalls.

Today was unprecedented, because it was the first time that I couldn't bring myself to go. The loneliness seemed to have defeated me. This was the first time I had accepted that there would be an unsuccessful ending to this annual struggle. I had given up trying to make a success of being part of something that invariably didn't want me to be part of it. There seemed no point in fighting this loneliness any more.

I felt the feather's heartbeat, and became warm from inside out. I blinked as my eyes glazed over and a haze of pink surrounded me, like a misty sparkle. *Was the feather comforting me? Did it have empathy, feelings?* A whole new concept opened up to me as I wondered about the core of the feather and what it represented. Starting to feel more tranquil, I muttered to myself, 'Well, I need to be somewhere at half five, so I may as well wander through on my way.'

The tang of the scorching pavement hit my nostrils as soon as I stepped outside, and I decided to catch the festival on the way back. It was 30 degrees now, and the 20-minute walk to my destination took me from my little street, left onto Silver Birch Lane, another left to Highburd Road, across a busy junction, and then along streets to the south of the city. I breathed in the scent of lavender and jasmine from the beautifully kept small front gardens of the well-to-do, and marvelled at the size of the lavender bushes in full bloom compared to the scrawny potted lavender in my back yard.

As I walked, I felt the heat from the orange brick walls as I passed. I put my hand out. Blimey, the bricks were hot! There were no trees on this stretch of my walk, and the scent of the flowers took me along the heated streets to a tree-lined avenue where the coolness invigorated me.

I took a different route on my journey back home, which would bring me out smack in the middle of the festival. The orange brick walls still gave off an unusual heat, and the smell of cannabis, washing detergent, and drains, hit my senses in sequence as I walked the short distance home.

As I turned a corner to walk past the shops on the high street, the young man was still there, crouching in his usual spot by the side of the chemist. I said hello, and he nodded. I had stopped asking him why he was there such a long time. He never answered. I had a look at the stalls on the high street and kept an eye out for anyone I knew.

It was really busy. A new band was setting up and doing their sound checks on the corner of the high street and one of the side streets which had been cordoned off. There were happy sounds, and the drink was flowing. I crossed the road to take a look at the band. It comprised a cellist, two violinists, and a guitarist. I stopped to listen as they introduced their first song. They were good. They reminded me a bit of Bob Dylan's *Desire* album.

I listened to their first two songs, but didn't see anyone else I knew, so felt a bit awkward and began walking back along the high street whilst looking at the stalls. As I came away from the main drag to walk home, a thought occurred to me. That knife I had seen the other day. It had been on my mind since the helicopter incident, and I couldn't stop thinking about it.

When I walked past the last stall, which sold vegan butter, jams, and spreads, I saw it again! This time it was embedded in the stall's wooden uprights. It was as clear as day... until I blinked, and then it had gone. I knew it wasn't just some random knife, but the exact same one. Why did I have to see this? What if it meant someone else was going to get hurt?

I must have been standing still, lost in thought, because I heard someone say, 'Anything you like the look of?'

'Uh... oh... um,' I stuttered. 'I'll have a jar of your peanut butter, please.'

I was searching for my purse when two police officers came up to the stall and promptly arrested the stallholder. As one of them read him his rights, I overheard that he was being arrested for an incident involving an assault on a man a few days earlier.

When I got home, I checked the date that had been given. It was the night of the helicopter.

I never did buy the peanut butter.

26
Shut up!

'If we walk and walk alone, who walks with us? Better to sleep than walk alone.'

I opened my eyes.

'Who said that and what did you mean?' I found myself shouting into an empty house.

Whoever it was, they had woken me up. Phew! I was saturated in sweat, felt stiff and cramped, and so heavy. Ugh, this was a disgusting way to feel in the morning. My feet were numb, and I felt like I had just been through days of physical hardship of some kind.

I steered my body to the bathroom, not knowing whether I would fall on the way. I just lunged myself forward and hoped for the best. Walking was so difficult andI had to hold onto the sink to lower and lift myself on and off the toilet. As I splashed cold water onto my face, I was aware of a presence to the left of me. But there was no-one in the house other than me. I looked for Tilly out of my bleary eyes, as sometimes her gentle footsteps made a noise that was disproportionate to her size. The noisy old Victorian floorboards creaked with their age, and some had dropped a bit from the weight of many a user over the years. But Tilly was nowhere to be seen.

This morning, I felt a sense of dread heading into the office; it was almost tangible. I had a funny taste in my mouth, and I was flushing. It must be anxiety. What else could it be? I told myself, as I walked the short distance from the huge main gates across the yard to the large doors at the far end of the loading bay. I had to have my wits about me there, because the lorries reversed so close to unload that there was not much space to squeeze between the sharp edges of the metal electronic doors that lowered themselves to the floor, and the empty metal trolleys stacked up somewhat haphazardly waiting to be taken back to town and loaded to capacity again. It was a continuous, never-ending, pipeline of goods from here to the houses, and from the suppliers to the main sorting office, and back again. In fact, if the office was to close for even one day, the parcels would start to stack up. I had an image in my mind of parcels piled high up to the ceiling and starting to spill out into the streets beyond, burying us all as they multiplied at pace.

I noticed that The Voice was quiet – something I didn't usually realise. In fact, I would go as far to say that I had no notion of The Voice if it wasn't there! Before this morning, I realised that I either had The Voice or I didn't; there was no in-between; there was no worrying that my antagonist might come... until now! This was the first time that I possibly felt anxious that The Voice might be malevolent! At least before this moment, I could have some peace of mind when there was no adversary! For goodness' sake, shut up! I told myself, as I walked into the unknown.

The noise of the office overwhelmed me as soon as I entered. The peace of the early morning was speared by the harshness of coarse banter, the radio blaring, and the jarring noise of the squeaking wheels of the trolleys full of oversized parcels. I walked past the sorting machine, avoiding the manager's office. I said good morning to those who noticed me and went straight to my work station. How I wished it was a normal, everyday thing to be invisible!

There were already sacks of small packets waiting in a row for me to sort, so I told myself just to get on with it. I felt cold, so decided to keep my coat on. Craig was at the fitting behind me, and I tried not to listen to the constant babble that he threw out of his mouth without seemingly thinking what it meant, or how offensive it was. Craig was a character indeed, and he got away with a lot because he didn't seem to have any awareness of how racist, sexist, and right wing his opinions were. He was either extremely stubborn, didn't understand, or very clever in a devious sort of way. I could never fathom him out!

I often challenged him, but today I just let his voice fade off into the background to join the many others. I wasn't in the mood to be at all sociable today, but unfortunately it couldn't be avoided for a few hours at work each morning.

With the realisation of the impending Voice, I was concerned. What if The Voice started to be objective, and I started to randomly spurt out the words that I heard in my mind? What if I said something I shouldn't? Was this what *people with Tourette's syndrome had to deal with every day? How did they cope?* The morning was a blur of instructions from my manager, with my mumbled replies of 'yes' and 'ok' and 'will do'.

It took me longer to organise myself to be ready to leave and go out to deliver. I wrote a list then lost it. The sooner I got out of the office, the better! No coffee, no break, I decided to just load the van as quickly as I could. In the end, I must have left the building about three times, forgetting this and that.

I finally left the office with dark thoughts of wanting particular co-workers to lose their jobs. But I told myself to stop thinking like that, as I would never want to lose my job. How would I pay the rent or eat? There were some people who were the most irritating idiots I could ever imagine, but who was I to judge? I got in my van and drove, arriving at my first destination without any further distraction. By the time I parked, I didn't feel too bad, considering the foul mood I had left the office in.

The Dis–ease was in my right foot today, and for about half an hour I was unable to walk in my usual way. For once, though, I didn't get as anxious or panic as I usually did, imagining that I had broken something and that I would be out of work and homeless, all in one foul swoop of ridiculous ominous prognosis. Instead, I carried on regardless of discomfort or pain, and soon it dissolved into just a twinge, before disappearing entirely. I now realised that I have to be given the physical nudge of pain to realise that I should have taken the good option to be able to triumph. I have to feel the physical discomfort in order to receive the nudge to wake up to the possibilities that making the right decision can bring about.

As I approached the corner of Bartley Road, the Walkie Talkie man was there as usual; same time, same place, every day. When you have a job like mine, you see the daily habits of individuals and get to know their rituals. There he was, wearing a navy padded anorak and sensible shoes, which the weather did not warrant today. A tall, slender man in his late fifties, with short greying hair, he was standing a few metres away from the outside of the corner shop. The shop was a local newsagent that sold most foodstuff, as well as the usual corner shop items. It didn't open until around ten am, which was a nuisance to me because sometimes it meant I had to visit it again on my journey back to the office. I could never understand why on earth a corner shop would open so late in the morning.

Walkie Talkie man stood, a carrier bag in one hand, containing items I presume he had bought from the shop, although I had never witnessed him coming in or out of said premises. His other gloved hand was up to his mouth, and he was furtively talking into a two-way radio of some kind. But it was just his hand! I watched him as he looked around with his eyes, not moving his head. He looked like someone who had taken the Official Secrets Act but had difficulty in concealing his stealth. He was surrounded by an air of uncertainty and the colour of iridescent blue. I wondered who he was having a conversation with. I always said good morning to him, and he would acknowledge me with just a nod. I'd never got close enough to hear any conversation.

So far so good, but The Voice did seem imminent. I tried to be more positive and noticed the flowers and plants in people's gardens, the insects, and the birds. This was a tree-filled area, with greenery all around. The dahlias were in full bloom. I noticed the sounds more acutely than anything. The birds were in full song, the zephyr brushing against my face, the sound of distant barking, and the sump sound of bags of plaster that a builder was stacking. Exchanging good mornings along the way, it was a sound-filled morning, full of enough distractions to keep me calm. I actually began to feel a squeak of excitement as I walked along.

'In these dark times you notice the blossom all around, but not the one visible in your own back yard!'

Shut the fuck up! I mumbled inside my mind. You're back then?

Was my adversary being sarcastic? This felt different; there had been a hint of positivity in that sentence. Hope, even! I saw a flash of yellow and pink, then orange and fruit cocktail, my favourite! But the colours were usually associated with the feather, not with The Voice!

Well, if that was The Voice, there's no way I was going to start taking advice from it!

This really was a living thing that had to be obeyed for my own self-preservation, to be able to survive! Talk about instant karma, I had assumed at first that the feather was just a mark, and not a mark of something else. I thought the heat that sometimes occurred was an effect of the (tattoo-like) mark on the skin. And even when it lit up, it took a while to sink in that it was actually a living organism within me! But did it control me? Or did it just react to me and my thoughts or actions? It really was a curse and a gift at the same time. And whichever way around, the overall result was complete control.

My phone rang and interrupted my ponderings.

It was Elsie. We had arranged to go for coffee and cake in the café in the village green a few streets away from her house. *It's still on then*, I thought, as Elsie could be unpredictable at best. I answered the call. This was a surprise; it was usually me checking up on her.

'You ok for later?' she asked.

'Yeah. I'll see you there at two-ish,' I replied. *Hmm, something's up*, I thought.

She was chirpy and relaxed when I entered the café, and was wearing a bright blouse and a colourful headscarf.

'Hiya!' she said.

'You alright?' I asked.

'There's a fab selection of cake on the counter,' she replied, looking over her shoulder.

She raised her eyebrows, and I gathered she wasn't talking solely about the variety of cake, as a rather handsome man was leaning by the coffee machine, looking at his phone.

'He's new,' she added, with an enamoured look on her face.

I laughed. 'Yes, he is rather dishy,' I said in a silly voice.

But I had other stuff on my mind. That sense of urgency that I get sometimes started to creep in while I was looking at the cakes. My stomach flip-flopped, and it wasn't the thought of a 'tasty treat', but that of a concern that I might be late and miss something.

'I am worried about my hospital appointment,' said Elsie, when I sat down. 'It's with the consultant, about my tablets. The thing is, I have the final show of my jewellery course on the same day, and I don't want to miss it.'

'Ohhh,' I said, realising it was Elsie's urgency I had felt.

'What do you mean "ohhh"?' she asked, with a confused but slightly paranoid expression.

'Um, nothing. Why don't you write down exactly what you want to say to the doctor and any questions for him, and then you can be more time conscious without worrying if you have missed anything out?' I suggested.

She nodded.

'You've got an exhibition then?' I said.

'Yes, we are exhibiting our stuff at the old gas works. It's full of trendy art studios now.'

'Nice one,' I said.

'It's the set-up and drinks with the class tomorrow, then on Friday evening it's the show. I have two tickets for you.'

'Great stuff,' I replied. 'That will be something to look forward to.' I really hoped the show would go well for Elsie. She needed a boost. 'Is "His Nibs" going?' I enquired.

She shrugged. 'Hmm, well, he is supposed to turn up at the opening, but who knows?'

Perhaps it would be best if he didn't, I thought, but didn't say anything. I just nodded.

'He better not turn up and make a scene,' Elsie grimaced. 'I'll throttle him. He's upset Nancy, and I am bloody mad.'

'Hope not,' I said. *He really was a spit-poison of a man*, I thought.

27

His 'Nibbles' and Wine

The opening, as Elsie had said, was in a very up-and-coming trendy area in a part of the old city, where a gas works had been converted into art studios, shops, and cafes. It had an 'industrial chic' design throughout, and I knew everyone would look smart and arty. I was hoping the free wine wouldn't be cheap and nasty, as it often was at these opening events. There was a bar, but a free glass of bubbly came with each invitation. I dragged Janet along with me, even though she said that she wasn't in the mood.

I knew that it would take her ages to get ready, so I made sure I told her that the opening was an hour earlier than it was. Even then, we got there late! I suppose it wasn't 'the thing to do' being early, or on time, though.

I was very impressed by the interior. It was the kind of place where you walked in, looked up and around at the architecture, and your immediate response was: Wow! The building was cylindrical and high. It consisted of three storeys connected by a circular stairway, which also had lights strung around it. The bar was downstairs, the exhibition was on the first floor, and the restaurant on top.

The outside was impressive, too. It was lit up by strategically placed lighting, and a building had been erected inside the gas-holder. It was amazing! Elsie's college had hired it out for the evening, for free, in return for a small percentage of the sales from drinks and food at the bar.

I looked round for Elsie and spotted her talking to a group of people by the bar. We walked over.

'Hi, Elsie,' I said.

'Oh hi, both,' she replied.

She looked bright-eyed and happy, and was wearing a beautiful dress that had been designed by one of the other artists. We both hugged and kissed her on the cheek.

'Congratulations,' we said simultaneously.

I hadn't seen her like this for a long time. Perhaps it was the champagne. Whatever the cause, I was glad. 'This looks amazing,' I told her, as we took our free glass of champagne from the bar.

'Let's go up and look at the exhibition,' Elsie suggested.

The three of us climbed the extravagant stairway, looking all around as we went. There were a lot of people there, so the evening was looking like a success already. I hoped that Elsie and the other artists sold their work. I didn't know many of the people, only a few of her textile mates that I had seen her with before. Her sister Sarah and daughter Nancy were also there. The exhibits consisted of beautiful textured wall hangings, jewellery, clothes, and ceramics. I became immersed in the colour, and as I looked at the different display cabinets, I felt my feather flutter.

Elsie had wondered off to talk about her work to a group of visitors, and Janet was enjoying the jewellery displays. A large wall hanging of Elsie's had taken my attention. As I looked, the colours leapt out. At first, it seemed too busy and confusing.

There was tartan, a hexagon pattern, and linear circles, pinks, lemons, greens, and blues. It was called 'The One'.

The feather flushed hot, and I started to sweat. *Why is it always my face?* I thought, as the sweat trickled down the side of my cheek. Suddenly I couldn't believe what I saw in front of me. Amongst the chaos of the pattern, a face had appeared. I concentrated on the image as the shapes and colours disengaged from each other and seemed to re-form. My stomach churned as I realised that the face peering out at me looked like 'His Nibs'.

I turned away for a second and blinked my eyes. Phew! That had been disturbing. In the hanging, the face had been distorted and looked in some sort of agony. When I looked back, though, it had disappeared.

I looked at my glass. I had only taken a couple of sips. *This is good stuff!* I thought, and drank the last bit quickly. Janet approached carrying two more glasses of bubbly with a quizzical look on her face.

'What's up?' she asked.

'Uhh...' I was just about to explain, when...

'Hello,' said a voice from behind.

I rolled my eyes, and Janet giggled. My heart sank as I turned and saw 'His Nibs' in the flesh.

'Hello,' we both replied; me somewhat nervously.

'What do you think?' he asked.

I knew that whatever I answered he would have a long-winded retort of his own unbelievably arrogant musings, so I just replied, 'It's great.'

Just then Elsie came up, thankfully. 'You're here,' she said.

'Well, yes, I was invited,' he replied.

'I didn't think you'd turn up,' she told him.

'Well, I did,' 'His Nibs' replied with a grimace.

I shivered. I really don't like you, I thought.

Janet announced that she wanted to go outside for a cigarette, so I said I would go with her. I needed some fresh air, as the bubbly had gone to my head. It really was good stuff. I had been sipping on it nervously and realised I had drunk all of the second glass. Going outside was also a great way of getting out of talking to 'His Nibs.'

As we walked away, Elsie mentioned that they were going upstairs for something to eat, and we would see her later.

'That was close,' I said to Janet as she lit up.

'What do you mean?' she replied, dragging on her cigarette.

'Well, I just get uncomfortable talking to him.'

'I see,' said Janet. She didn't really know him like I did. 'Are they still together?' she asked.

'Oh, who knows?' I said. 'It's on-off, on-off. I've stopped asking.'

We decided to go back in, have one more drink, another quick look around, say our goodbyes, and go and eat in The Lounge on the way home. It was far too expensive to eat here, as Janet had pointed out earlier after studying the menu. The drinks were a fair price, too.

But before we could open the door to go back in, Elsie burst out of the entrance, red in the face with what looked like anger.

'She's here!' she shouted.

'Who?' I asked.

'That bitch he's been seeing.'

'What?' I turned to Janet, who looked bemused. 'What on earth! I can't believe the cheek!' Words failed me. 'Did she come with him or just turn up?' I asked.

'I dunno,' said Elsie. 'I gave a few flyers out at the kids' school. She either saw one of them or came with him. I wanted to knock her out there and then. She's with a few friends of hers that I know from school, some of the mums. The nosey bitch.' She seemed to calm down a little and added, 'He looked quite surprised, actually, but he went over to talk to her!'

'What you gonna do?' I asked nervously.

'I'm not leaving. I AM GOING BACK IN!' Elsie shouted.

'Well, try and stay calm,' I advised, knowing this could be an impossible feat.

'Come on then,' Janet said. 'Let's all go to the bar.'

Elsie walked back in with an air of 'challenge me if you dare', and we followed.

The feather had started to constrict, and the skin around it felt taut and uncomfortable. All I wanted to do was lie in a bath of moisturiser.

When we got back inside, 'His Nibs' was at the bar, but Elsie's demeanour changed as she smiled and bought him a drink.

I felt very confused.

28
To the Dogs

Wind me up and throw me out. To the dogs, I go, wretched and fearsome to all. Then reel me in as I blink in the light of my ugliness and guilt-ridden aftermath; for all to see the bitterness of my soul in grief and humility.

Talk, talk, talk. There was an incessant rambling inside my head.

There had been no warmth, no glow of colour in the feather lately. It was a time of anxiety and depraved thoughts of bitter revenge. Some people were getting my goat! So much so that I had started to become nasty and gave them back even more than they had dished out. Just to be certain that I could finish the job in one clean, even sweep, I stamped their criticism, mistakes, and selfish sarcasm into the ground. I had become bad, and for a very short time, it felt good.

'Don't ever make an enemy of me, it won't bode well!' I mumbled to no-one in particular.

The only thing that I was scared of was myself. I could harm someone, horribly, and swipe their lives out in an instant! The violence I sometimes felt knew no limits! I could, and would, kill or maim with my bare hands. I knew that I was inherently both good and evil, but it's not like I had a little angel on one shoulder and a cute devil on the other, like in the cartoons. If that was the case, I would listen to both and form an educated decision. No, this was something else! I knew that The Voice was evil and the feather was good, but both could take control of me at any time.

It was all-consuming, and I found it almost impossible to control the evil that could exude from me when The Voice was at the forefront. This wasn't doing me much good, though, and I knew that if I continued on this course, I would become physically ill. I had to be in the best of health in these unprecedented times, for the sake of myself and others.

On these occasions when I allowed The Voice to run free and unguarded, the consequences were disastrous for all concerned. The feather was black – not raw umber, not French navy, not dark grey, but black – with a streak of blood-red on the tips. I felt a stinging pain and a gloopy treacle substance had started to leak from it. *Was the feather dying?* I wondered. My t-shirt had stuck to it. *I hope this comes out in the wash!*

'Is that all you can think about, whether it will come out in the wash?' The Voice pondered, knowing I was listening.

'Blimey, it sounds like you have a conscience,' I replied.

Perhaps I should give 'It' a run for its money? Beat it at its own game. Be worse than it could ever be itself. More destructive than it could ever imagine being. But that could either encourage The Voice, feed it, or scare it off. Was I bold enough to risk the consequences, whatever they may be? That would show it! I would need to feed off The Voice's words to start this process off, then flip it around on itself! Did it have a slight conscience somewhere in the darkest depths of its being? Perhaps the feather was starting to influence it.

My phone rang, and jolted me out of my procrastinations. The pressure was too much, so I had started to enjoy not answering it. I found satisfaction in knowing the longer it would ring, the longer I wouldn't answer. I was enjoying the thought of someone not getting their needs met. Besides, I was working. Did people think I was on call for them 24/7?

The feather now seeped a dirty grey. It reminded me of a time when I hand washed my clothes, and the disregarded water that smelt as it slipped down the plughole.

I was angry! In general. With everyone! Especially 'His Nibs'. Not only was he trying to mess with Elsie's head, but now he had started to involve me. This morning, another message from him had been passed on to me via Sal, one of my co-workers. The message was that 'I didn't do very good accents at all!' So, what was that supposed to mean?

'What did he mean?' I demanded, feeling confused and startled.

'I don't know!' Sal replied defensively.

'Did he say anything else?' I said sharply.

'Nope,' said Sal. And with that she added, 'See you later!'

I just stood there as Sal walked away, and felt the anger boiling up inside me. It came quick, like bile bubbling to the surface.

'If you're going to pass a message on, I think there should be some sort of explanation,' I mumbled. Like, how did he look? Did he seem annoyed, psychotic? Not just some flippant sentence and walk away! I winced as the feather felt uncomfortably hot. Now it had turned crimson colour to match my face as I marched outside for some air.

Sal had been delivering on the street where the 'other woman' lived, while I had been temporarily covering another area. So 'His Nibs' must have been looking out for me. How dare he just pass a stupid, possibly threatening, message onto me through a co-worker like that! I was livid! I saw a dirty tar hue spread around my body, before it dissipated into the air. Sal was a complete stranger to him! Had he seen me and Elsie go to the café that time? I wondered. Was he spying again? It wouldn't be the first time! I wished that I hadn't had to see him at the exhibition last Saturday.

I trudged back to the office, still fuming from the morning's revelations. It was unlike me to stay furious for that long!

Freddy was just back from delivering, and sauntered into the car park, took one look at me, and said, 'Do you want a coffee before you go?'

'Yes, please,' I grunted back.

Freddy was a good friend at work, and he always had my back. I think he secretly had feelings for me, but I didn't have the time or energy for any kind of relationship beyond platonic these days. He grabbed some change and headed to the coffee machine.

I am just going to ignore the paranoid ramblings of a narcissist, I told myself as I waited in the yard. Should I tell Elsie? I wondered. No, I won't, because then she would realise that I bump into him often, and she'd want me to pass on messages, or even worse, spy on him. No, no, no, I think not. This had started to get out of hand, and I did not want to get embroiled in the paranoid world of 'His Nibs' and Co, as there would be repercussions which I couldn't handle.

I had also started to worry that 'His Nibs' had accomplices. There had been a couple of people who I had seen a few times now around the area of the 'other woman's' house. I felt surreptitious looks in my direction from these dodgy geezers, who seemed to be just ambling up and down, past said abode. Did he think that I had rung him up and pretended to be Irish, or French, or even Scottish? Why on earth would I do that? And for what reason? Did he have such a high opinion of himself that he thought I would waste my time, and my energy, on even thinking of doing such a thing? Was he receiving phone calls from his enemies? Or maybe other jealous women putting on different accents? Had it been Elsie messing around? Who knew? There were numerous possibilities, and I just couldn't be bothered to think about it any more.

Today had been a bad day, and as Freddy handed me a coffee, we sat under the smoking shelter and discussed the day's events. He told me that a customer had accused him of somehow losing a parcel of theirs, and how he had told them in no uncertain terms that they wouldn't be getting any more deliveries from him again! Now, if I said that to a customer, I would have instant karma and be reported. I can't seem to do or say anything that's derogatory without a comeback. How do some people get away with it? Is it because they think they are right to say these things, and do just that with such confidence that it results in no consequences? Or does my feather keep track of all my misdemeanours?

We talked about this morning in the office when Craig, another co-worker, had been immensely irritating. He had been talking a load of crap, spouting ridiculous derogatory stuff about other nationalities. When Craig opens his mouth, I mostly think, *Shut the fuck up!* But today I had actually said it out loud.

'Oh, shut it, will you?' I had shouted. 'You sound like a fucking Nazi!'

There had been giggles all round, but Craig had looked surprised and piped down. Five minutes later, he threw a packet of sweets on my desk. Then I'd felt guilty. But Freddy laughed and said that Craig had deserved it, as he was becoming more of a pain each day.

Later on in the morning, Craig had been just putting some parcels in the back of the van, when I had an impulse to push him in, watch as his face slammed down on the floor of the van, and lock the door! *What is wrong with me?* I'd berated myself. *I could injure him in some way.*

I knew this was no good for me, but I had lost control. The Voice had won for the time being, so I went with it. *Oh, I know I am going to regret this,* I told myself. *Dear God, why do I do this to myself? How can I stop these random thoughts of violence and negativity?* Perhaps I shouldn't have left the house today. Perhaps I should get home and lock myself in my room, but even the thoughts I was having would eventually escape and cause harm.

I had to be strong and tell The Voice that enough was enough. When I feel down, The Voice knows that I am vulnerable or tired, and takes advantage of the situation. It waits for me to let my guard down and swoops in. *What if it has accomplices?* I wondered. *Surely it can't be ready waiting, watching 24/7? How does it stay on top, all this time, knowing that there will be an opportunity to pounce and take my mind from me, so that I don't know what I am doing, and then it's too late?*

I went to the ladies' toilets and tried to wash the day away, but marks had started to appear on my face, showing the ugliness within. I couldn't bear looking at myself in the mirror any longer. Boils had started to form on my chin. Was I being punished for past misdemeanours? Or was this my alter ego which I was finding difficult to control? Or was I supposed to feel this way so that I might be able to help others with their experiences? I was struggling with feelings of being unable to control darker thoughts and behaviours, not knowing how to feel about anything. Not knowing if these were the feelings of others, or premonitions of similar situations happening to other people at the same time. Multitasking to the expense of saneness, or not, as the case may be. Feeling joyous because of the talent that I possessed, but scared of the consequences of my own thoughts and behaviours. To be evil is easy, to be good is hard. I was not taking the easy way out.

I had also in some way annoyed Lisa. I wasn't exactly sure why, but at a guess, it's because I didn't follow up on a phone call. I have a habit of saying that I will do something or make promises to people, then I forget. They are only things like 'I will ring you' or 'I'll message you' at a certain time, or on a certain day. But I just forget.

And it's not that I don't care. It's just that I have so much going on in my head that some of it invariably gets lost in the mish-mash of tangled thoughts, scenarios, and anxious feelings. Even when I get an offer of help from someone, and I say I will ring them about it, I don't. You would think that when you have worked it out yourself and there's no need to bother them with it, they would be pleased. But no, they ignore you or are put out in some way. It's like I can't do right from wrong.

Why does everything I do have such a strong, rippling effect on those around me? I may as well just lock myself in a room and not speak to anyone. What is it that makes people expect so much of me? Why do people react in such extreme ways towards me? I have lost patience with people who randomly react towards me in a way that I have absolutely no idea where it comes from. I feel weighed down by my own thought process.

I felt better after the coffee with Freddy and left for home. Tilly was waiting for me in the street. I love it when she welcomes me home. At least the cat gets me.

Feeling exhausted, I put the kettle on for a cup of Earl Grey; I couldn't have coffee again so soon. I turned my DAB radio on, set at Classic FM. There was a Schubert Impromptu playing, and for a moment it grabbed me in its clammy hand, holding onto my heart. It was beautiful; it made me feel so sad, but yet hopeful. If I went under now, so many people would be affected and I couldn't do that to anyone, especially those I love dearly.

'Don't deny even the most tentative power,' someone said.

I felt the feather glowing, and I smiled weakly.

29
Is This Real?

It had been a week now since the show opening at the gas works, and I hadn't heard from Elsie. Overall, the event had been a success, and at the end of the evening an announcement had been made that a lot of works of art had been bought or reserved, so everyone was pleased. Elsie had sold one of her wall hangings for a good price. Surprisingly, 'the other woman' hadn't stayed long, and Elsie and 'His Nibs' seemed to be getting on – mostly at the bar drinking.

I remember feeling different during the last part of the evening, as if something was not quite right. As soon as we had gone back in after Janet's cigarette and Elsie's announcement about the other woman, things had seemed different. It was like I was watching from a different place, and seeing everyone play a character from a different scene of another play. It was certainly an experience that felt familiar, but then I couldn't quite put my finger on it. As I watched the night's events unfold, I felt that the daily foibles of the human being were alien to me somehow. It didn't feel natural for me to be human. It didn't feel a natural thing for me to have the emotions of a soul within a body.

On the way home, Janet and I stopped to eat at The Lounge, and I felt much better. Perhaps I shouldn't have been drinking on an empty stomach.

When I got home, I felt that sleep was imminent, but as I lay down and closed my eyes, I only felt a sigh of comfort and relaxation for a few seconds until the uncomfortable, inevitable fight to stay awake. I haven't felt the same since that night.

I remember the time when I was around 11 or so, and a stray dog with a limp followed me all the way to the animal sanctuary, which I happened to pass on my way to a mate's house. I hadn't even realised that there was an animal sanctuary there until years later, because the entrance was two large gates covered in sheet metal, with an intercom to buzz for attention. There was a sign outside, but it was high up, and I had not noticed it because I was rather small for my age.

As I passed the entrance, a man was just leaving the sanctuary, and said thank you to me. Consequently, the dog was scooped up in his arms. It was like water off a duck's back to me. These serendipitous events were an everyday occurrence, although at the time I had no idea. I took things at face value then and never questioned anything.

I thought that I talked to myself a lot because no-one else listened to me. And I realise now that the feather is the only thing or one that does. The feather has told me to own my own power. I must have been talking to the feather all along, but nowadays, I am noticing the signs on a deeper level. I am able to do something about them and act on them... well, sometimes. I question to try and understand. Now I almost always know when a sign is being shown to me, but in the past I hardly ever understood. This is advantageous, because now I know how it could help me quickly, sometimes instantly;

enough to take action immediately or in good time, depending on the situation.

Time is passing at its usual pace, but the signs are coming faster. Because of this, I could achieve the things I want to, and will be able to help others. The possibilities are endless. Could I warn people or even save an injury before it happens? Pre-empt situations? Yet I have to fight constantly not to give into the dark and go with it. The feather keeps me safe but The Voice tempts me. I could go either way. The balance is crucial.

It's such hard work keeping myself fit in body and mind. The fine tuning that is required is infinitesimal, and that's just to keep relatively fit and on an even keel. How on earth athletes do it, I will never know. Every niggle is connected with every thought. As I walk the tightrope, I get the impression that it's been greased on certain sections, daring me to slip off. But if I glide over these areas and ignore the uncertainty of it all, I find I can walk with purpose as the days unfold. If I don't think and just get on with it, then everything trundles along nicely.

30

The Mirror

Everything seemed clearer today, as if the world around me had been generally sorted and spring cleaned. The atmosphere felt different; that is, until I entered the second block of flats in Aspen Close! In the first block, I had the feeling that there were no walls. I could easily have been at a beach on a clear autumn day, or walking through a field with nothing but sky and no buildings to enclose me. The euphoria of a still calm lake only lasted a few minutes. It was just a glimpse, but most enjoyable and memorable.

I got to the second block of flats, and I clambered over a large puddle of urine just inside the entrance. There was a gloopy mess on the stairs, a dirty, stained mattress, a used nappy, and a small swarm of flies! The lift was also stuck, so I climbed the first three flights then gave up and left. Even so, I didn't let the unpleasant surroundings get to me. Walking felt easier today, like I didn't have to make any effort at all. The hills and steps didn't tire me. I felt taller, like a giant who could cover large distances with its massive gait. The sun was out, and there was a positivity in the air. People smiled and said hello, and it wasn't raining.

I moved onto the next part of the delivery, to a café where I could use the facilities and buy a snack or a drink.

'You don't have to buy anything to use the toilet, you know,' said the owner with a smile.

'I know,' I said. But really, I thought it would be rude to just use the loo and not buy anything. I always bought something that I needed anyway, even if not at that particular moment.

I ate a Mars bar in the van before I moved on. They were smaller nowadays and gone in two bites, yet I remember they were too filling for me when I was small.

At the junction, I looked to see if the road was clear, but the driver of the car to the right of me was doing the same. We both looked right then left, and right again, but we were in each other's way and our eyes met. It was difficult not to keep looking at each other, and she smiled. She looked familiar. In fact, I couldn't keep my eyes off her. What was this strange feeling that had started from my toes and worked its way up, like an electric charge, but not of a nice kind?

We were identical!

It was like looking in the mirror!

She signalled to me to pull over onto the next road, so I did. Goodness knows why this complete stranger wanted to talk to me. But it seemed only natural as I got out of the van, and she walked over to me.

'Hi,' she said, with a smile.

'Hello,' I replied.

There was an uncomfortable pause. I tried to think of something to say and could feel myself going red, and then she spoke.

'Umm, the reason I asked you to pull over is because I can't help noticing that we look very similar.'

There was silence. I tried to say something, but I stuttered, and the words just wouldn't come out.

'Were you adopted?' she asked.

'I… no,' I replied, shaking my head.

'Oh. I was,' she replied in a matter-of-fact way.

Words had definitely failed me, which was kind of unusual.

'May I take your name and phone number?' she asked.

'OK,' I muttered. But I didn't really want this woman to contact me and be disappointed when we were not related. She was definitely searching for family.

Did she have a feather? I wondered. But I didn't dare ask.

The euphoria of the day had been blown away like sand on the shore. I could almost feel the energy drain from me, and suddenly I felt disgruntled.

'Ok, thanks,' she said, as I gave her my number.

We both realised we were responsible for a build-up of traffic as our parked vehicles were contributing to an already busy area near a school. As we both turned to get into our vehicles, she called out, asking if it was ok to ring me this evening. I said, 'Yes, ok.' But as I drove off, the disparity of my mindset grew to almost unbearable anxiety.

Was it too late for me to achieve what I needed to achieve, or what I wanted to achieve? Was I ever going to be able to do this? It seemed like life was preventing me from doing what I wanted. Why did life and the need for money to exist, thwart me? Around every corner, distractions seemed to dupe me and prevent me from continuing with my purpose. I felt maudlin, anxious, frustrated, and tired of all the necessary red tape of life! If I were to live in squalor, I would have more time, but then the surroundings would not be conducive to the art.

Later that evening, the woman did as promised and contacted me. We arranged to meet at a café near to where our paths had crossed. Her name was Gemma.

31

Water, Water, Everywhere and Not a Drop to Drink (they were the best of times, they were the worst of times)

I often think that things couldn't get any worse. Oh boy! But they can! When I think that life can't get any harder and it suddenly does, then I wish that I had made the most of it when it was what it was! Therefore, I have decided that I may as well go with what I have at all times, whether good, bad, or indifferent, because the situation can always change. I have vowed to myself to always enjoy the moment, because there is no other. Then at least I am making the most of it before it gets worse, or before it gets better. Either way, it's all I have.

It had been three weeks since I heard the news that 'His Nibs' was dead; not from Elsie, but from my ex.

I had replied with the usual disbelief. 'How? Where? And when?' My stomach had curled up when I first heard.

He said he wasn't sure, and that no-one seemed to know, or if they did, they were not forthcoming with the information. The more questions I asked, the less information I seemed to be able to gather. It was as if no-one wanted to let on. I asked my ex to find out as much as possible, because Elsie wasn't answering her phone, even though I had left umpteen messages and texts.

The very next day, I had driven to Elsie's straight from work. The cats were about and obviously being fed, and her car was on the drive. But that was no clue as to whether she was in, as she often walked places to save petrol, and sometimes her car wasn't running. She tended to buy cheap run-down vehicles that didn't last, as money had always been tight for Elsie.

I had also driven past the other woman's house, but no-one was outside. I couldn't quite believe it somehow. It was frustrating, and after a couple of weeks of non-stop calling Elsie, turning up, and texting, I gave up for a couple of days, thinking she would come to me if she needed to.

I was considering going to visit her mum and dad, but if she was there and wanted peace, then I could be intruding. My relationship with Elsie had become exhausting to me. Had she done a runner? Was it an accident, or a suspicious death? An overdose? Who knew? Someone must, but I decided I'd had enough of trying to find out. I had a life of my own to lead and could not waste any more time.

Then the very next day, there was a message on Facebook, saying that the details of the funeral arrangements would be announced soon! I texted Elsie and she answered straight away, so I rang her quickly before she disappeared off the face of the earth again!

'Elsie, I've been trying to get in touch with you for two weeks now! I've been so worried. What happened?' I demanded.

'I know,' she said. 'I couldn't talk. I've been sleeping at my mum's and just going back in the day for the cats. That bitch and his family have been making all the funeral arrangements.'

'So, what happened to 'His Nibs', Elsie?' I asked.

'Someone took him to the hospital and then left without saying who they were. He had a reaction to something he had taken. Some drug; not sure what. Because we weren't married and that whore got there first with the family, they wouldn't tell me. I think she poisoned him.'

'What? Why do you think that?' I said, as my feather raised off my back. I felt sick.

'There's a post mortem going on, no results yet.' Her voice was strained, and she sounded distant.

'Shall I pop by after work?' I didn't know what else to say.

'Not today,' she said.

'Ok, let me know when you're up to it. We could go out for lunch. Let me know if you need anything.'

'Ok.'

32

Late Lunch

I did meet up for lunch a few days later; not with Elsie, but with Gemma. It felt like a cool October evening, when in truth it was coming up to 3pm in September. It seemed odd; it was a Sunday, but it felt like a weekday, and there was something in the air. I sensed some excitement as I walked down the high street heading home from meeting Gemma in The Lounge.

I felt a bit guilty, because I had been preoccupied and had met up with Gemma a couple of times whilst Elsie was in hiding. But I felt calm and secure in her company, as we both listened to each other. I decided I didn't care if we were related or not. I wanted to remain friends either way.

The Lounge had been packed out and quite noisy, but it was good to catch up with her for a chat and some lunch, with quite a lot of caffeine to keep the chatter going – not that we needed much help. It is described online as a 'scruffy-chic bar with a cool vibe, vintage adverts, terrace, and an international comfort-food menu'. And it does have a lot of atmosphere. I feel at home there, as it's one of those places where you can forget that you are not at home.

The customers are a mixture of different types of people, who sometimes bring their children while others bring their dogs. There are obscure portraits on the walls, and a lot of low-hanging lighting with kitsch lampshades. There are cushions, too, but I like to avoid those, as sometimes I can see the germs or micro-organisms that no-one else seems to see or think about. I always go for an upright chair, usually one with a seat that can be easily wiped clean. I was surprised when I looked up online about germs on cushions, that they actually can live on hard surfaces longer than on fabrics! But I still don't like them.

I had now met someone like me! Gemma and I seemed to share the same feelings and the same thoughts. I spoke with her for a couple of hours or so over coffee, and it seemed like we had known each other for a long time! She talked about past feelings, and the difficulties she had faced whilst overcoming events in her life. She told me that she had been adopted and was now looking for two siblings, and discussed her feelings of loss and grief, not knowing who she was and how she fitted into this world.

I could identify with her. It was as if she had sat in front of me and described my feelings, issues, and behaviours over my entire life. The only difference was that she had stayed in a terrible relationship with the father of her children. She told me that her young daughter was currently undergoing treatment at the hospital. They were staying together for their daughter, and not for themselves.

I listened mostly while she let off steam. But my emotions rollercoasted for an entire afternoon as my life flashed before me.

33
The Burial

The street was busy, and so was the pavement. The church was one of those one-storey, modern buildings, with numerous large, elegant windows. There were groups of very different people, or that's how they looked on the outside, anyway. It was like the Olympics. There were the hat-wearing, smartly dressed, gospel-singing Christians, the laid-back Rastafarian crew, and the everydayers, or miscellaneous (which I was a part of). There was a very elegant man dressed in red, gold and green. He wore a beautiful sage green cloak, and carried the Jamaican flag. Last, but not least, were the family (which was a mixture of all the groups).

It was tense from the outset. I arrived with my ex, who had known 'His Nibs' from years before. The reception committee comprised two of the hat-wearing Christians. It was tightly organised, and a lovely young man handed me an order of service. I had a quick look into the church. It was like an auditorium, with layered seats down to the stage. There was no sign of Elsie.

She had told me she was going to sit at the back, away from his family. My ex was chatting to a group of people he knew, so I went back to the front area and hovered by the entrance.

There were a few faces I remembered, but was not on familiar enough terms to go and chat with. I felt like a spare part, or a teenager not knowing what to do with their arms. Then finally, some people I knew arrived – a few of Elsie's family and friends. We all looked out for her.

After a few long minutes, Elsie arrived with her sister and daughter. She looked bad, mad, stern, and bereft. In fact, there were too many different emotions exuding from her. I felt nervous. She looked like she might explode, and it was taking all her energy to hold it in. We greeted each other, but she was distracted and looking around. She was looking for the other woman, and there was a possibility from previous conversations that another unknown woman could also be there. Elsie wanted to identify her. *How?* I wondered. There were so many rumours going round, but I knew that Elsie had her own way of getting to the truth.

We all entered the seating area and Elsie went straight to the last-but-one row, ignoring the ushers completely. Nobody was going to tell her what to do today! We (Elsie's mates) sat either side of her like bodyguards. There was an unwritten rule we were all abiding by. We all knew that she needed protecting from herself more than from anyone else. My ex sat with his nephew and the Rastafarian crew in the two rows in front.

Elsie was quiet, but still urgently looking around. Then she pointed out the other woman right at the front, near to his close family. Her face reddened and I could almost feel her blood starting to boil. One of Elsie's friends made derogatory comments, and Elsie started to answer and agree, but in a very loud way.

'Please don't let this kick off,' I muttered to myself, as if saying it out loud would make a difference. Nothing stopped

Elsie in her tracks. There was no-one who could control that temper of hers.

I sat in silence, inwardly cringing at the remarks Elsie and her friend were making. While the ushers were showing the last of the stragglers to their seats, I could see the tension in the shoulders of the congregation who were within hearing range.

I thought about the circumstances in which 'His Nibs' had died. The death certificate seemed shaky to say the least. 'Unknown' was in there somewhere, but I couldn't quite remember the exact words.

'*Did she poison him?*

'*Did the other known woman, or one of the unknown women, poison him?*

'*Did they all get together and kill him off?*'

I told The Voice to shut the fuck up, this was a funeral, for goodness' sake!

For all his sins, Elsie still loved him desperately. If there ever was a time to control my mind, it was now! The feather was pulsating, its colours drab, with splashes of red and black. The Voice was muttering.

'Come onnnn!' I said out loud.

Oops! People looked round. I pretended that it was normal to shout out at a funeral, and eventually after some stringent, bemused, confused, and tormenting looks for what seemed like a lifetime, people turned back round, muttering and murmuring. Elsie actually giggled, and the rest of the row just ignored me.

The service went ahead without a scene, and thankfully Elsie stayed seated. But her friend was quite vocal during the service and would randomly voice her opinion on what the speakers were saying, with an accompaniment from Elsie. They both talked loudly enough for the surrounding rows to hear. I imagined that everyone in this funeral wanted it to pass without a hitch; each person, knowing what 'His Nibs' had been like, would regard that as an accomplishment. He was very popular in his death, as well as in his life, but for different reasons. In his life, people were scared, or at least wary of him. In his death, there was still tension, and a lot of unanswered questions.

As the coffin was carried out, we all left to drive to the graveside, which was a short distance from the church. But no-one seemed to know the directions, so we relied on our sat navs or phones. We started to follow each other, but the traffic was not conducive to a convoy. When we finally arrived at the graveside, there were already a good hundred or so people milling around. This time, Elsie was at the graveside, scanning the area.

The men dug the grave, taking it in turns – something which I had never seen before. The hat-wearing Christians sang gospel songs. It was heaven to my ears. After a while, Bob Marley songs were blasted out from a CD player. The atmosphere was electrifying, and I felt like the feather was strong enough to lift me off my feet. The colours were beautiful now and the feather was fluttering. So was my heart.

'Here we are standing together, what do we represent? We represent ourselves; each other to a certain degree, but we mostly represent the Divine Love of God. As we stand, our energies intermingle and proclaim the universal core of what is mostly observed by our loved ones who have gone before us. They can see us more clearly than we can see ourselves or others who are in a physical body. From their higher perspective, the true love and desires we have are laid out, as are also the detrimental effects we can have on ourselves and the people around us. They can see our true colours, literally, colours emanating around us, reacting

to the slightest change in circumstances, the outside influences and effect that others have on us, as we go through this physical life. Their desire to help us is somewhat confounded by our inability at times to see or feel past or through our physicality, even if we realise we are energy before we were encased and born into our physical bodies. We can forget this and be downtrodden in the day-to-day sudden dramas of our physical life. Divine Spirit tells us and informs us subconsciously or consciously by a perfect connection directly to ourselves, our spirit. The connection is so strong and yet simple, and pure and delicate in its viscosity.'

The other woman stayed further back, as it was Elsie's turn to rule the roost. Now she was in the open air without the constraints and formality of the church, she stood stronger than ever! But now it was more dangerous, and anything could happen. Elsie pointed out to me who she thought might be the unknown woman. She had a name but not a face.

One man started dowsing the grave with frankincense – my favourite scent – whilst the others sang. The aroma filled the air. There was also a strong smell of weed, and someone sprinkled some bud onto the coffin. 'His Nibs' would need a last smoke to take him into the next world, I heard someone say. There was a short burst of laughter, which broke the tension – for a short while, at least.

As the grave was dug deeper, the songs became stronger and more soulful. Some women started to wail loudly. Some were talking in tongues. I looked around and noticed that the most prominent women in his life had gathered closer to the graveside. There were now two opposing groups, standing opposite sides of the grave, facing each other, all looking round from one to the other like a gang of meerkats, waiting to see who would make the first move. There was nowhere else to look.

I was standing next to Elsie, but began feeling uncomfortable about the looks I was receiving. It felt like they were summing me up and wondering if I was one of his women.

'Well, he certainly didn't have a type of woman; anything goes.'

Move on! I told The Voice.

Finally, the coffin was lowered into the ground, and the men took it in turns to shovel the dirt back in. *One Love*, by Bob Marley, was played. No singing this time. Elsie shouted out that it was not his favourite song, and that the funeral was a farce, but no-one else said a word.

We left with Elsie. There wasn't a wake – at least, not one that we were invited to – so we all went to Elsie's local and had a few drinks.

34
Seeing Clearly

Buy one, get one free, my arse!

I left the opticians feeling robbed! Yes, my new frames looked good on me, like I had a brain of sorts, but come on! That was extortionate! My eyes had deteriorated so much in just under a year that I now needed new lenses, so I had decided to buy new frames, too. No wonder I had been constantly cleaning my lenses, thinking they were dirty. It was my inability to see, not the cleanliness of the lenses. Anybody would think I was stupid, the way I go on. *I can't be that thick, can I?* Perhaps that's what people think of me. *I mean, I do get some bizarre reactions from people, don't I?*

'*To whom are you talking?*' said The Voice, in a bored, stuck-up tone.

'Not you,' I said, 'so mind your own business. Ok!'

At least I'd had my eyesight sorted before my break away.

The walk down to the coast took concentration, and the walk up took my breath away. The sea was warm and made me smile, but there were jellyfish. It was a gentle distraction and relief to catch up with a dear friend who I had known since the age of 16, to touch base and be able to keep a constant in both our lives. We were important to each other, but not demanding of each other's time.

It was a beautiful September evening, warm enough for a dip in the sea, even though it was the Atlantic. The headlines in the local paper had said the summer had been reminiscent of the 'summer of 76', of which people had fond memories of the school holidays stretching out in endless hot days, swarms of flying ants, and sitting on the outside windowsill of their houses, listening to Stevie Wonder playing live in the vetch field a few streets away. I had wished for that type of summer for a long time, and this year it didn't disappoint.

As we clambered carefully down the rugged steep cliff steps, some too smoothed by the sea for my liking and my sandals, Alison was telling me about her latest exhibition in the north. We reached the bottom and I looked out onto the bay; it was as beautiful as it always had been, and I thanked nature for all its glory. The sea shone a cobalt blue, and we went straight to the edge of the water, ready for our dip. There were two young girls chatting and relaxing just ahead in the sea, their conversation coming towards us like two birds on the breeze. A few stragglers were heading home, and a dog was sniffing around, its nose to the sand, checking out the debris that the tide had left, with no humans near enough to know who it belonged to.

We relaxed and chatted as we slowly made our way out, snagging our feet on the pebbles beneath. I didn't like to go too deep, as there was always a nagging fear of a shark lurking further out, or maybe something that I couldn't see in the undercurrent.

I remember as a child my mother demanding that I must not go too far out and that it was essential I swam between the red and yellow flags which the lifeguard had placed, usually around 30 metres apart. Almost always whilst enjoying myself,

I would be gently shifted by the tide so that I was outside the flags, and I then had to make my way diligently back into the allocated area.

We saw many a jellyfish washed up on the tideline – three different types: a small translucent moon jellyfish; a tiny purple type called a blue; and some sea gooseberries. We didn't know enough about them to be sure of their stinging capacity, so we looked out just in case. The sea felt like a beautiful, warm, summer blanket wrapped around me, with an early evening temperature that had built up all day. It was wonderful!

The sun was low and shone strongly on me. I felt a hugely satisfying grin spread across my face. Oh, what a feeling of release! But it was short-lived. I saw a large blue floating towards me, and our sea adventure was cut short. We exited quickly! There never seemed to be this number of jellyfish when I was little, unless I just didn't notice. I didn't care. I felt so relaxed, more than I had in a long time. No work for two weeks, and some time away just to be myself.

'You don't know how to be yourself, because I say what you think.'

I just ignored The Voice. Tomorrow I would be going to a caravan for a week with the girls, and I had my mind on just enjoying life.

We said our goodbyes, and I left Alison on her doorstep, waving me off, before getting ready to take some of her prints to a gallery in London the next day.

I needed an early night in preparation for my car journey. But I was too excited to sleep straight away, and woke up feeling tired. At least I was packed and ready.

I had a strong cup of coffee, fed Tilly, and kissed her goodbye before setting off to the caravan, where I was meeting the girls. The endless stretch of motorway, combined with the droning, monotonous sound of the tyres on the road, could produce instant sleep for me, so I had to stop for a flat white or cappuccino every one-and-a-half hours, and eat sweets or chocolate to keep me from disastrous consequences.

Tilly had been catered for, as my ex was looking after her. I had left strict instructions for her needs – some ridiculous, as he pointed out. I needed daily pics sent on WhatsApp of her, and he was to kiss and cuddle her intermittently throughout the day. I knew he probably wouldn't, and left trying to pretend I was just popping off to work, as I didn't like the wrench of leaving her. She had a few scabs on her ears and some tiny patches of fur missing from her paws. Ex said it was the rose bushes which she clambered in and out of, but I was worried that Cat no. 3 was bullying her.

The caravan was great. It was clean and had the necessary functions. We just read, walked, ate and drank, and did whatever came to mind. The temperature was warm to hot, but not unbearable, although it rained most evenings. Our days usually started off with a trip to the beach.

We took a slightly different approach to our daily walk to the sands one lunchtime – later than our usual ten o'clock start (well, we were on holiday!). There had been persistent rain for a day and a night, so the path was a slippery and muddy journey of tentative steps as we tried not to land on our behinds. To avoid the worst of the mud, we took a small diversion by cutting through Seaview caravan and small chalet park, past the noisy, well used pool, and through a driveway consisting of a worn-out fridge, two manky microwaves, a piece of piping, which looked like a forgotten part of a sink unit, and a piece of worn rubber. There was also an old Mini – French navy, my favourite colour – and a rather new-looking caravan, the modern type ready to be taken on a family holiday somewhere, gleaming, waiting expectantly to be drawn away.

As we made our way back on our usual path, which was a straight cut through a woodland area, I saw the warm breeze brush and rustle the soft leaves of this Indian summer. But I didn't feel it. Janet was silent by my side until the path only allowed for one, whilst Jenna was singing the 'hokey cokey' some metres ahead. Elsie was behind, occasionally voicing slightly controlling orders to slow down, or to watch the muddy steps.

I wondered what Elsie must be thinking. She had been quiet most of the week, almost reverent, especially in the evenings when we usually went out to eat, or if tired, ate snacks in the caravan. None of us could be bothered to cook, even though the caravan was well equipped for such tasks.

Elsie had given strict instructions that we must not talk about 'His Nibs' under any circumstances. We had all agreed on this, even though there were times when we took turns in slipping up, by mentioning something pertaining to him or the subject of what would happen next. Elsie didn't often come out for drinks with the café girls, but they had met her on various occasions over the years, and we were a pretty easy-going bunch.

Behind our caravan, there was a beautiful view of the farmer's expansive land, sometimes with a drove of bullocks, before the cliff dropped to the sands below. One morning, as I looked out to take in the pleasant view, I saw the bullocks in a circle. They seemed to be surrounding a blue object lying on the grass. I went out to take a closer look and discovered that the object was a body board. I giggled to myself, as I imagined a bullock body surfing.

An occasional yacht or a one-off cruise ship would sail by, but on the whole the campsite was a quiet, unassuming place, consisting of one field of caravans, neatly moored side by side a good enough distance from each other for privacy to be maintained, but grouped in a circle around the perimeter. We were at the top corner and had a spectacular view.

If it didn't rain in the evenings, we sat out for a drink and chatted, watching the view, feeling tired and sun-kissed. Jenna, as usual, drank too much. She would say that she only wanted a couple of drinks, but once that bottle was open, there were no limits. I was always the first off to bed. It was a way of getting time to myself.

Often, at the beach I would say I was going for a walk, promising to stop for refreshments on my way back, leaving the others reading or sunbathing. Today, as I walked along the beach with my feet in the sea, I felt euphoric, and I thought about how far I had come. I remembered the dark times when I couldn't see any way out of the quagmire I was in after the birth of my son. I had loved being pregnant! Thomas was born on the 12th of March – a day I remember well. He was born to classical music from the small radio in the delivery room.

I had wanted a baby for so long, but was just 20 years old when he came into this uncertain, beautiful, exciting, dangerous, and exquisite world. I was so proud to hold him in my arms, and had a huge grin of relief on my face when they wheeled me back down to the ward. I had happily let the midwife fuss over him and check he was all right. Prior to that, I had sworn that no-one would take him out of my sight. He arrived to the sound of heavy, intense, dramatic classical music, and the labour was the same. I remember the midwife asking me if I wanted her to change the channel on the radio to something more cheerful, but I said that it wasn't necessary. Little did I know that the music would be symbolic of how it was to be for a while afterwards! At one point, I was off my face on gas and air and asked why there was a packet of ham on the wall.

I thought that the depression afterwards was like a blanket that would never be lifted. I imagined that was what I would feel like for the rest of my life. Everyone else knew it wouldn't last, but I didn't. Everything seemed so hard. The exhausted feeling became a burden. It prevented me from thinking, doing, living, seeing, and being. *Where was my life going?* I'd wonder. I was nowhere, my brain was fog, and I felt depressed beyond knowing what I was. When I was told I had depression, it didn't mean anything to me, all I knew was that I was in oblivion and didn't understand how this had happened.

I was struggling to survive, to cope with my baby, to want to get out of bed in the morning, stuck in this nightmare, wanting to be left alone by the outside world which didn't seem to understand me. It felt like a continuous world of disparity where nothing made sense and there was no way out, ever! If only others would let me sleep, that's all I wanted to do, but there was no let up. What was the point? What a waste of two years in that depressed state, wasting time away.

At any moment, life can change dramatically. It only takes a series of unfortunate events, and life can feel so intolerable that it's not worth living. But then again, it only takes a series of fortunate events to turn a life around for the better, to end up in a place of pure happiness and joy.

I knew there was something else, something else that I should be doing. This wasn't a new thought that had just recently entered my mind, and it wasn't one of my realisations. I had known this from the moment I was born, but without knowing. I could say that my unconscious mind knew but my conscious mind didn't, although it wasn't that simple. *But what was it?* The feeling had become stronger as each year passed, through my degree that I loved, through the job that I adored, through the struggle to go alone. This deep, nagging desire within me to find out what it was that I should be doing. *Was it connected to the longing that I had throughout my childhood, the feeling of the painful longing to go home? What was it?*

I know now that living for the moment is the only way, although it's taken me years to understand this. Glimpses of the realisation have appeared throughout my life, but never remained long enough to have a lasting impact on me. It's painful even to think of that time, but now I can look back and thank so many people for their help. After wanting my baby for so long, it had been devastating to be in that state of mind.

Then one day, I had been walking along the street, pushing my son in the buggy, when I felt a click in my brain, like a synapse had physically moved! I felt the pain very briefly, but it was not really pain; it was more a movement, like something had snapped into place physically in my head. And that was it! I immediately felt as if the fog in my mind had cleared within seconds! I was different; the depression had gone.

I will never forget that feeling. It was as simple as if someone had pushed a button or clicked a switch. *Had someone been pushing my buttons?* I thought of an Iain Bank's novel where people were controlled by others under the ground, like glove puppets physically having their lives controlled by a series of connections. In retrospect, I wondered if the depression was an experience that I had needed to feel. It had lasted too long for my liking. *But was it for a reason?* It was something I could only know at a later stage of my life.

By the time Thomas reached two years old, things were great. Not all the time, but mostly.

'Thomas is his own man now. He is happy and making his way in this world.'

'I know!' I said, then paused. 'Who said that?'

I looked around. I don't think anyone heard me. There were people in the sea, but I was at the water's edge. I decided to carry on walking until I reached the rocks at the far side of the cove, and then make my way back. My face felt taught, and I needed to reapply some Factor 30. I continued strolling, still deep in thought.

It had just been a statement, but it hadn't sounded like The Voice as it wasn't sarcastic, cruel, or annoying. *Yes, Thomas is making his own way in the world*, I thought, and smiled. He was studying Physics at Uni.

'Goodness knows where he gets his brains from,' The Voice jeered.

'And there we go,' I spat.

Thomas had moved in with his dad when we separated. He had been quite mature for 15, and the decision was easy for him as he and his dad had always got on well. Living there was also closer to the sixth form college he would soon be attending. Even then, I saw him a lot, as he would pop by for his tea every other day or when his dad was at work.

That precise point in time when I heard the click and felt the movement in my head was the day when a new chapter had opened up for me. I didn't know it at the time, but the constant revelations I had started to be aware of then became 'the norm' for me. My feather felt warm and had started to glow!

However, staying completely in the light could leave oneself more vulnerable to the dark. Being completely of the light, when disrupted, can bring disappointment of the utmost heart-breaking, horrifying death to your soul. When your light is crashed through or infiltrated by darkness, it can feel devastating. You have to know a bit about the dark to be able to protect yourself from it. One can be trained all one's life for a special purpose without realising it. All the parts of the jigsaw are passed on by each person, happening, or symbol, from all different sources: whether they be animals, humans, events, thoughts; even inanimate objects can bring inspiration. The purpose of this is to help you on your journey, whether you realise it or not. Each event or person is put in your pathway to veer you off course, or to direct you as the crow flies, sometimes to quicken your way, and sometimes to distract you and delay, but always in the end leading to the total.

Suddenly, I saw a fluttering out of the corner of my eye. A feather was floating down from the sky. Its colour was green, but forever changing; first turquoise, then lime, sage, blue, yellow, and pink. The colours were iridescent. I felt light, and so did the feather on my back. A warm breeze enveloped me, and I could smell the warmth of the sun and the freshness of the sea.

I reached the point where the rock pools held their warmth. It was time to turn back, so I moved up the beach a bit and walked along the tideline, looking for shells or pebbles that caught my eye. I took a deep breath, trying to get every ounce of sea air deep into my lungs until it hurt, then slowly let my breath go, releasing the old stale and putrid thoughts that had gripped my soul. Out into the atmosphere they went, where they were blasted with the positive particles of the sea spray, then swept away into nothing.

It was the feather's day today, not The Voice's, and I knew that it was gently steering me in the right direction. As I looked out to sea, I noticed a tiny speck of light flickering and bouncing along the wave that was building up. Everyone was getting ready to ride this wave, body boards poised, prepared to mount as it grew larger, building momentum, waiting to jump on the board, just after the crescendo, before the break of the wave took them speedily to the shore. That feeling of the rush and force of the water.

The light still flickered, but became red and agitated as it bounced from peak to peak of the choppy waves, until it finally rested on a young boy. He was poised, waiting to enjoy the ride. As the wave broke, the lad jumped onto the board too harshly and his body slipped off to the side with the force of the water. I watched, frowning, as the board flew up in the air, cut by the wave and the relentless energy of the sea. The boy disappeared, and I became anxious. It felt for a moment like the feather had jumped off my back!

Where was he? I looked over to the lifeguard, who seemed to be scouring the area but didn't seem concerned in any way. My heart was pounding as I rushed to see if the boy had popped up somewhere else, looking for his board. I called to the lifeguard and pointed to the area where the board was still floundering on the waves. He began to realise something was up, but I was already rushing into the sea, fighting the tide.

My legs felt heavy and too slow, so I swam towards the board. Then I saw the boy just under the surface of the water, and grabbed him round his waist and lifted him high. The lifeguard was right behind me, and took the boy from me.

Where were his parents? He was far too young to be left to ride those waves by himself. I looked around while the lifeguard carried out his duties. The boy was coughing and spluttering, but ok by the looks of it, thank God.

Better get those drinks back to the girls.

33

The Lost Girl

I stood and waited. Good job it was a sunny day, so that I could cry behind my sunglasses. There was no shade in this position, so it was a good excuse to wear them. I didn't attempt to walk through the small group of people who were milling about outside, as that would have seemed inappropriate. There was no rush, so I stood alone a short distance away, and waited.

There was no sign of Gemma. She had been trying to get in touch with me on the last day of my holiday, but the phone signal had been intermittent at the caravan, so there were several urgent messages waiting for me when I arrived home. The next day I had woken early to meet her.

After a short while, I thought I had better move a little closer so as not to seem so unconnected. Then there was a slight movement as people stepped aside to allow Gemma to walk through. She looked dazed as she came towards me. I threw my arms around her, and she sobbed. I felt a flutter of anxiety in my stomach. My feather ached, but somehow felt full of colour waiting to be unleashed.

As I held Gemma, she tried to say something, but the words were lost through her tears. A priest appeared at the entrance of the hospital, most elegant in his robes; white, with a green and yellow trim. He looked anxious, as if he had lost someone and needed to find them quickly. He seemed familiar to me somehow.

Then the father appeared, conveying the same anxious look, desperately scanning the area. The small group were in turn looking around and starting to whisper to one another. There seemed to be a state of confusion.

Gemma was holding on to me, sobbing desperately, but I realised after a few seconds that everyone was looking in my direction! The father was rushing towards me, with the priest a few seconds behind him, both beckoning for me to come with them.

'Is she the one?' the father shouted.

'Yes,' said the priest.

'She was standing alone earlier?' asked the father.

'Yes,' the priest insisted.

I looked behind me to see if I had misunderstood; to see if there was a person standing at my back, but there was no-one. They both looked at me expectantly. For the life of me, I couldn't fathom out what was unfolding, but their need was so great and all-consuming that I went with them both, after a woman had gently persuaded Gemma from me.

I followed them through the group of people and into the hospital foyer, down one corridor, then left down another and into a ward. I didn't look at anyone; I just wanted this to be over. *What on earth could they need me for?* I wondered.

To the left of me, in my peripheral vision, I saw and heard people weeping in a room off the ward, but didn't look directly at them. I started to come to a halt when I saw a curtain drawn around a hospital bed in another side room. My stomach lurched; I didn't want to intrude on anyone's grief. I felt my breathing become more difficult, and I took a long inhale and a few short exhales.

My mind was swirling with thoughts. *Surely, they would soon realise that they had the wrong person for whatever they needed?*

The sweat started to trickle down my face, and I felt an intense heat throughout my body. The feather glowed. It felt sore and uncomfortable. I wished someone would explain to me what was happening, but there didn't seem to be any time, as the sense of urgency seemed to be all around me, closing in on me.

'Come, come,' said the priest, and with an air of irritation he put his hand onto the top of my shoulder and ushered me into the small room. The three of us entered, and the priest shut the door behind me. There was a nurse standing there looking at me. She seemed as confused and anxious as I did.

'What's going on?' I asked the priest.

I felt my breath quicken as I spoke. When the words left my mouth, they seemed to change tone, and it didn't sound like my voice. I felt disconnected to my body somehow, and found myself silently asking the feather for help – something I hadn't thought of before.

The father and the priest looked at one another pointedly, then back at me.

The father said, 'Listen, I need you to bring my daughter back to life.'

There was a pause…

'Sorry?' I gasped.

'I know you can do it. I just know.'

The nurse had tears in her eyes.

After some stuttering on my part and some shaking of my head, I said, 'She's gone... her spirit and soul lives on, but her physical self cannot come back to life! It's not possible!'

I felt like I was watching this scene from a distance – whether above or beyond, I neither knew nor cared; I just wanted out.

He made a sudden movement towards me and grasped my hands in his. 'Please, just put your hands on her body,' he pleaded. 'You must help!'

The priest nodded kindly.

I was half dragged by the father to the bedside, then the curtain was drawn back, and there was the little girl, looking beautiful and at peace.

'Put your hands on her,' pleaded the father.

'Ok,' I found myself saying, in a complete state of disbelief and shock. There was a gloopy shield between me and the others as I held the little girl's hands.

Hasn't her spirit already left her body? I thought. *She's passed away!*

'Her beautiful spirit would have left her body by now,' were the words that I cried, as I spluttered through my tears. 'She will live continuously in peace. She will be looked after. Family who have gone before will be waiting for her.'

'I was told earlier that you were the one,' stated the father in a harsh tone.

'The one what?' I blurted out in anger and disbelief.

What is this ridiculous farce? I wanted to shout. But I stopped myself as I became aware of a beautiful blue white light that had started to build up around me, spreading quickly to envelope everything in this little space! I felt lighter, as if there was no gravity.

I put my hand on the girl's shoulder, and as I did, she moved!

We all gasped.

'Listen,' I said, though it did not sound like my voice, 'there are three options: The first is that she stays in spirit and lives there, where she will be able to grow up with no disability; second, she could come back to the physical, but there are still possibilities that her health will continue to suffer; or she can come back to the physical, where she will be fit and healthy and all her disabilities will disappear—'

'The last one!' the father interrupted.

'But there is a condition,' I continued. 'You and your wife will not be able to stay together because of your child any more. It is not fair on any of you.'

'Anything,' said the father, who was now on his knees in desperation.

At that moment, Gemma came bursting into the room, but then stepped back with a look of shock and disbelief. She made a gulping noise, and I thought her heart might stop. She held onto a nearby chair to stop herself falling.

The little girl started to move her hands and stretch her fingers, then opened her eyes as if someone had just saved her from drowning by chest compression. She coughed as the breath of life came back into her lungs. The light subsided, and she was helped up by the priest and taken to her mum, whose outstretched arms grabbed her and held her tight.

'Mummy, you're squashing me,' she said.

As all three embraced, the priest turned to me and asked, 'What on earth are we going to tell them all out there?'

'I don't know,' I replied, 'but there is going to be chaos soon, so would it be ok if I slipped out the back?'

'Follow me,' said the nurse, smiling.

We left the room, and the nurse very quickly led me to a door. 'Thank you so much,' I said, as I opened the door. And before anyone could stop me, I began running... and couldn't stop.

As I ran, I thought about Elsie. I had an overwhelming need to go and see her.

36

Goodbye Elsie
(Expedient)

After a few minutes, I ended up speed walking the rest of the way. My legs were not made for running. My need to get to my destination was not matched by the speed of my physical body, and I swerved around people and corners, almost losing my balance a few times, and tripping over my own feet. Regardless, I managed to stay upright. My calves were cramping, and the feather felt tender.

Elsie's house was about three miles away, but I didn't remember the journey. When I turned the last corner into her road, I saw a group of people in the distance. I couldn't make out if they were gathered outside her front garden. As I drew closer, I could hear my heart pounding; it was painful. The events at the hospital seemed aeon's away as I struggled to get to her door. The scene before me was somewhat bizarre.

Quite a crowd had formed. The neighbours opposite and on each side of Elsie's house were on their doorsteps, and there were loud voices offering assistance to Elsie and her daughter. There were three police cars in the road, and two officers were escorting Elsie from her doorstep to one of the vehicles. Elsie's daughter was already in the first car, looking solemn but calm. There were a few friends talking to her through the open window. She nodded to me. Somehow, I knew that she knew there were no words, and that we just had to let the scene of events unfold. There was nothing to do.

Elsie, on the other hand, wasn't going to go quietly. She did what Elsie did, and any interference from another person would invariably make things worse – usually for the poor person who tried to help. I had given up trying to give any kind of advice or help when Elsie was in one of her moods. I had learnt the hard way, after receiving many a harsh dismissal of any advice freely given.

'You can bring a horse to water, but you can't make them drink.'

That felt too comforting to be The Voice, I thought.

Elsie was always right – well, in her opinion – and the best way forward was to do absolutely nothing to try to console her in any way. Now she was shouting obscenities to her neighbours as she made the short distance to the open door of the police car. Something about 'twitching curtains' was all I heard.

Someone called my name, and as I turned, I was surprised to see my ex coming out of Elsie's house. I didn't understand why he was there, but there was no time for questions. I frowned at him before turning back to watch helplessly as my friend was being taken away.

I couldn't understand what had happened to Elsie. She had become bitter and twisted, and all that life threw at her seemed to be just too much. The loss of close loved ones in the past, a lifetime of grief, an abusive relationship, and her health issues on top of that, were enough to have pushed anyone over the edge.

Elsie had become more and more angry, withdrawn, and secretive over the last few months. And now she was being escorted into a police car by two officers. As I watched Elsie being dragged away by them, I could hardly catch my breath through the tears. My ex put his arm around me and tried to persuade me to walk back to his car. Shrugging him off, I distanced myself from him and waited as they finally pushed Elsie into the police car.

I wanted to shout something comforting to her, but the words wouldn't form on my lips. As she struggled against the officer, she turned her head and shouted out to me, 'Anna!'

'Yes?' I cried, between panicked breaths.

The policewoman had her hand on the top of Elsie's head now, trying to finish the difficult task of getting her inside the car.

Elsie yelled, 'I have a feather!'

'Whaaaat?' I said, aghast.

My heart pounded, a searing pain filled my chest, and I found myself holding onto Elsie's garden fence. I felt my feather start to rise off my back, and I needed to take a few short breaths. I had to let go of the fence; the pulling force was overwhelming.

Suddenly I was looking down on the scene as if watching a film. I was flying! A sense of calm filled every cell in my body as a searing blue light came from ahead, through the air, towards me, encompassing and reaching every part of me. I looked down at myself and realised that the colour was emanating from me.

I watched in amazement at Elsie struggling as she resisted and tried to back out of the police car. A comical scene unfolded. Elsie was half hanging out of the car while the policewoman tried to prevent this, her face red and a slight panic spread across her eyes. The policewoman was half the size of

Elsie, and Elsie had fight within her, whilst the officer looked like she had had enough already. Several other officers on scene rushed over to assist her.

I fought to get back down to the ground.

'Elsieeeeeee!' I shrieked.

But before I could continue, Elsie screamed wildly, 'It's complicated!'

There were now three officers using all their strength to push Elsie back into the vehicle. I couldn't look.

Doors slammed, engines revved, and all three cars sped away. Then she was gone.

**

I can understand the concepts of light and dark. I can understand why it is easier or harder to be persuaded towards each side, depending on the circumstances, the feelings, or the ideology. I can even understand giving into something that you know is wrong, just to be spiteful, vindictive, bitter, or twisted. I tried it, and it didn't work for me, or anyone else. It's trivial to pursue any revenge. Once a moment is gone, it is gone. Why let it burn inside? Especially after a cooling off period of time. Forget it and move on. But what if it is something as insurmountable as murder, tragic death, love, torture, or abuse to oneself or someone you love. It's not as easy then, is it? Having strong emotions is never easy. Then you have to make a decision. Which do you go with? The dark or the light?

We are both in prison now! I presume Elsie had chosen the dark over the light. Me? Well, I keep fighting to stay within the light, because my imprisonment is the darkness all around.

**

I slept and slept for England and for Wales, maybe even for Scotland. Or further still. I don't know if I wanted to wake up – well, not in the physical body, anyway. The feather came to the forefront, and The Voice had faded into the background. The feather had now absorbed The Voice, and it spoke of a time when I was all energy. The time I had been longing for. The time I had cried for when younger. The time I remember, but don't know any more. I had not yet been born into the body I wear now.

The feather was pleased with me, and now I was the feather. We had become one. I felt lighter than I had ever done before, and knew I had come home. I knew I had received the mark before I was born; it had grown with me. It had started off as a birthmark and formed into a beautiful image of what I could be.

Acknowledgements

Thank you to all my friends and family, and to the following people and organisations:

To Michael Heppell, who lit the spark to finish what I started, for all your knowledge, encouragement and endless enthusiasm on your 'Write That Book Masterclass.' Thank you to the members of the masterclass, and to my accountability group called 'The A-team', for constructive feedback, helpful discussion, and good company. To Anndreea Sandu for much needed extra technical support.

To my amazing publishers Kim and Sinclair Macleod, Ann and team at Indie Authors World, for their enthusiasm, expertise, advice and support.

To my editor Christine McPherson and proofreader Jenny Williams, for their patience and knowledge..

About the Author

I am a postal worker by day, but have many projects which I work on the rest of the time. I am from Swansea and now live in Kings Heath Birmingham. My passions are fine art, writing and reading anything that takes my fancy.

For many years I taught life drawing and painting classes. After my daughter was born, I took time to write down my thoughts, and any spiritual philosophy that popped into my mind. This started my pathway to becoming a medium, a spirit portrait artist and a healing medium at Kings Heath National Spiritualist Church.

I am writing this book under the pseudonym Lyn Benzino. It is a fiction novel that has many underlying truths within it.

Find me at:

featherofmanycolours.uk.

@lynbenzino for instagram .

lyn.benzino@btinternet.com.